"My Secret Baby With The Billionaire"

An Age Gap Second Chance Romance

Olivia Mack

Copyright © 2023 by Olivia Mack - All rights reserved.

In no way is it legal to reproduce, duplicate, or transmit any part of this document in either electronic means or in printed format. Recording of this publication is strictly prohibited and any storage of this document is not allowed unless with written permission from the publisher.

All rights reserved.

Respective author own all copyrights not held by the publisher.

Contents

1. Chapter One: Sophie   1
2. Chapter Two: Jared   14
3. Chapter Three: Sophie   28
4. Chapter Four: Jared   41
5. Chapter Five: Sophie   54
6. Chapter Six: Jared   68
7. Chapter Seven: Sophie   82
8. Chapter Eight: Jared   96
9. Chapter Nine: Sophie   110
10. Chapter Ten: Jared   124
11. Chapter Eleven: Sophie   137
12. Chapter Twelve: Sophie   150
13. Chapter Thirteen: Jared   164

14. Chapter Fourteen: Sophie — 177
15. Chapter Fifteen: Sophie — 190
16. Chapter Sixteen: Jared — 204
17. Chapter Seventeen: Sophie — 217
18. Chapter Eighteen: Sophie — 232
19. Chapter Nineteen: Jared — 245
20. Chapter Twenty: Sophie — 258
21. Chapter Twenty-One: Jared — 271
22. Chapter Twenty-Two: Sophie — 284
23. Chapter Twenty-Three: Jared — 299
24. Chapter Twenty-Four: Sophie — 322
25. Chapter Twenty-Five: Sneak Peek — 339

Chapter One: Sophie

"What do you mean you can't find Cameron? You guys are supposed to be getting married in four hours."

With a sigh, I wince and pull the phone away from my ear. "Okay, Mel. I'm going to need you to calm down because I only got about half of that."

"He was supposed to stop by the apartment to pick up a few things, including an extra shirt in case he sweats. You know he sweats a lot."

I frown and wheel my suitcase behind me. "No, I really didn't know that. I could've lived without that piece of information."

"How can you joke at a time like this?"

I push through the glass doors and am met with a blast of hot air, raising the hairs on the back of my neck. With one hand, I cradle the phone between my neck and shoulder, and with the other, I move the suitcase.

I come to a stop on the edge of the sidewalk and glance down both sides of the street, eager for a glimpse of a taxi.

Heat rises from the asphalt and shimmers. The afternoon sun is high in the sky, and I've already sweated through my shirt. But none of that matters.

Not when my little sister's wedding is in a few hours, and she's having a meltdown. When I find Cameron, I'm the one who's going to give him a piece of my mind.

"....do you think he could be having cold feet?"

I squint into the distance and spot a cab, crawling forward at a snail's pace. "I honestly don't know, Mel. I thought the two of you were doing well. Did it seem like he was having second thoughts?"

Out of the corner of my eye, I see a flash of movement. An older man in a suit with some salt and pepper hair steps forward and blocks the cab door.

His phone is pressed to his ear, and his back turned to me as he yanks on the door handle. With a scowl, I slide in after him, set my suitcase on my lap, and slam the door shut with a thud.

"Mel, I'm going to have to call you back." I end the call and twist my body to face him. "You can't steal my cab."

He turns to face me, a furrow appearing between his brows. "It doesn't have your name on it. This cab is fair game."

"I don't think so. I have a wedding to get to."

"So do I. And you were on the phone."

"So were you."

He puts his phone into his jacket and faces me completely. Suddenly, I notice two things at the same time.

One, he's incredibly attractive with an angular jaw, almond shaped eyes and dark hair with some gray hair, which made him look even more attractive.

Two, his custom-made suit costs more than I'll ever make in this life. It does little to hide the broad shoulders, and the lean, muscular body underneath.

Holy hell. He is the most attractive man I've ever seen. And I can't decide if I want to chew him out for trying to steal my ride right from under my nose, or if I want to lean forward and kiss him squarely on the lips.

Before I can decide on either of these options, he reaches into his pocket and pulls out a wad of bills. "Why don't I give you something for your trouble?"

I glare at him. "I'm not interested in your money. I need to get to the hotel, so I can find my sister afterward. And if you have that much money, why are you even taking a cab? You can have your own private driver pick you up."

He sighs. "Well, I like taking a cab sometimes. Life is not always about choosing the most comfortable way, aaand...mmmm....my driver is stuck in traffic. Why don't we share the cab then? I'm going to the Westin Piedmont hotel."

"So am I."

"Fine."

"Great."

The driver, a bald-headed man in a Hawaiian shirt with pit stains and a protruding stomach, shrugs and eases away from the curb.

Through the glass, I see cars whiz past in either direction, tall and gleaming buildings glistening in the distance.

It feels strange to be back after all this time. Leave it to Melanie to bring the family back together out of the blue.

I shift and squirm underneath the suitcase. I pick my phone up and send Melanie a quick message. Once she responds, I sigh and press my face against the cool glass.

"We could ask the driver to pull over, so you can put your bag in the trunk."

"So, you can tell him to drive off? I don't think so."

"You really have trust issues, don't you?"

I swing my gaze back to his and raise an eyebrow. "So, you're telling me you haven't thought about it?"

"The thought did cross my mind." His lips twitch in amusement, a strange glint in the depth of his hazel eyes. "But you've gone through all of this trouble…you must really love your sister."

"I do."

He flashes me a smile and holds his hand out. "I'm Jared."

I hesitate, then hold my own hand out. A jolt of electricity immediately courses up my arm. "Sophie."

"It's nice to meet you, Sophie."

"I would say the same, but I'd be lying."

Jared chuckles and continues to hold my hand. "I like a woman who isn't afraid to speak her mind."

"I like a man who doesn't steal cabs."

Jared releases my hand and sits up straighter. "It looks like we both have strong opinions."

"I guess so."

My skin is still tingling where he touched me, and I can't get over it. *Get a grip, Soph. I know it's been a while since you've been with a man, but you can't throw yourself at the first man you see. No matter how good looking he is.*

Because I didn't have time to be distracted. I have a groom to locate.

We spend the rest of the ride in silence, my fingers moving furiously over my keyboard. Once we pull up outside the hotel, I get out of the cab first, the suitcase falling onto the pavement with a clattering sound.

I scowl and bend down to pick it up. When I wheel around to pay the driver, he's already driven off, joining a slew of other cars headed in the opposite direction.

Jared has a small bag at his feet and is messaging someone.

"How much do I owe you?"

Without glancing up, Jared brushes past me and up the stairs to the hotel. "Don't worry about it. I owe you for trying to steal your cab."

I scowl at his back. "So, you do admit it."

At the top of the stairs, Jared pauses to flash me another smile over his shoulders. I try to ignore the butterflies in my stomach as I race past him and into the carpeted lobby.

I wheel my suitcase over hardwood floors in the direction of the main desk, where a group of uniformed men and women are sitting.

As soon as I'm done checking in, I take my bag and hurry to the elevator. Before the doors ping shut, I catch a fleeting glimpse of Jared.

He's leaning casually over the counter, a small but playful smile on his lips, while a uniformed woman stands across the counter from him, clearly captivated by his presence.

I roll my eyes, and the elevator door pings shut. On the fourth floor, I get out and hurry down a carpeted hallway with doors on either side.

Once I reach my room, I swipe the key card and grope for the switch. Yellow florescent lights blind me as I kick the door shut and dial Melanie's number.

"Okay, I'm at the hotel, and I'm on my way to you now. Are you at Mom and Dad's?"

"I called his friends. They're searching everywhere for him."

"Have you tried his mom? You mentioned that he likes to go there sometimes."

"I didn't think of that. Soph, you're the best."

"I'll be there soon."

With that, I hang up and change my clothes. An hour later, I am driving Melanie around in her wedding dress, the windows of Mom's Prius rolled down and soft country music playing in the background.

We are circling back to our parents' house when Melanie receives a call and breathes a sigh of relief. "Okay, they found him at his mom's. Apparently, he fell asleep, and his phone ran out of juice."

"At least it wasn't cold feet."

Melanie adjusts the folds of her dress around her. "Oh, I'm still going to give him a piece of my mind. After the wedding."

I reach between us and squeeze her hand. "Atta girl."

Melanie sighs and stares out the window. "Do you think I'm doing the right thing?"

With a frown, I pull to a stop outside our parents' house and kill the engine. I twist to look at her and raise an eyebrow. "You're asking me for marriage advice?"

Melanie turns so she's facing me completely. "Well, yeah. Who else am I supposed to ask?"

"You could ask mom or dad. I don't think I'm the best person to ask about this, but yeah. You and Cameron are a good match."

And he did strike me as the kind of man who is going to stick around through thick and thin.

Melanie and I might want different things out of life, but I want her to be happy.

I push the car door open and spill out. After a brief pause, Melanie does the same and stands in the middle of the sidewalk in her wedding dress and lifts her gaze up to the sun.

The door to the house bursts open, and our parents emerge in the doorway, in a suit and lilac dress, respectively, wearing identical anxious expressions.

Once they see us, they wave us over, and I steer Melanie in their direction.

As soon as we step in through the door, everyone breathes a sigh of relief. Suddenly, we are surrounded by family and friends on all side, many stopping to greet me and pull me into hugs.

I keep an eye on Melanie who is swept upstairs and into her old room where her friends are already waiting. I stay downstairs for a few more minutes, making small talk until my sister calls out for me.

When I go upstairs and see her sitting in a chair facing her dresser, I wrap my arms around her for a hug. "You're going to be fine, sis. This is going to be a great wedding."

Melanie nods and smiles. "I'd steer clear of Aunt Josephine if I were you. She's been talking about setting you up with her accountant."

I chuckle and release Melanie. "Maybe he won't be so bad. You know I have awful taste in men."

"He's like three times your age," Melanie whispers, pausing to glance over her shoulders. "I've seen him. Trust me, you'll thank me for this later."

Before I can respond, our cousin sweeps in, with her hair piled high on top of her head and reeking of a pungent smelling perfume.

Melanie and I exchange a quick look in the mirror and smile.

As soon as she leaves, I wave my hand in front of my face and close the door to her bedroom.

"It's time for more important stuff."

Melanie stands up and smooths out her dress. "Like what?"

"Please tell me you've reconsidered the edible lingerie Aunt Christine got you."

Melanie throws her head back and laughs. "Don't even remind me. I'm going to be thinking of that every time I see any edible set."

I giggle. "I think that's the point."

We both laugh out loud.

Chapter Two: Jared

I lift the glass up to my lips and scan all the people, spilling out into the spacious backyard and dancing underneath the shade of a willow tree.

Music fills the air, coming from the live band set up on a makeshift stage.

Half the guests in attendance linger near the buffet in the back, studying the hefty spread with interest. The other half is dancing barefoot on the grass, their laughter slicing through the air.

Bright lights are strung up over the trees and bushes, and a crescent-shaped moon hangs in the middle of a starry sky.

With a shake of my head, I down my drink and signal for another.

Seated at a table in the back, I have a bird's eye view of my son, who is swaying to the music in the middle of the backyard, his arms wrapped around his wife's waist.

She has her head tilted back and is looking at him with such love and adoration that it makes me doubt myself.

I've sworn off love and women. But I can tell that Melanie and Cameron want to go the distance. At least I haven't passed on my cynicism to my son.

I cast another glance and spot a familiar figure hunched over the bar.

Sitting up straighter affords a full view of her side profile, a jolt of recognition courses through me. With a smile, I push my chair back and button my jacket.

I weave in and out of the crowd until I'm standing directly behind her.

"You know, it's bad manners to drink alone at a wedding."

She turns and pauses with the glass halfway to her lips. "You've got to be kidding me."

"I'm really not." I lean over the bar and motion to the bartender, dressed in black and white. "What are you having?"

She turns in my direction and sits up straighter. "A vodka martini. Are you stalking me?"

I raise an eyebrow. "I wouldn't be a very good stalker if I came up to you, would I?"

Sophie's lip curl into a half smile. "No, I guess not. Seriously though, what are you doing here?"

"I could ask you the same thing. Didn't you have your sister's wedding to get to?"

Sophie looks surprised and pushes her dark hair over her shoulders. "This is my sister's wedding."

I pick up my drink and tilt it in her direction. "This is my son's wedding."

Sophie's eyes widen into saucers. "You're Cameron's father!? You're Jared Fox!"

"Yes."

Sophie blinks and studies me. "You were late."

"Someone tried to steal my cab."

Sophie sputters and narrows her eyes at me. "No, you stole my cab, and we weren't late when we got dropped off at the hotel."

"Agree to disagree."

Sophie raises an eyebrow. "You were late to your own son's wedding."

"Guilty. Whatever you've heard, it's all true."

A flush steal across her cheeks. "I haven't heard anything."

I am fairly certain her sister has revealed a few things courtesy of my son.

Out of the corner of my eye, I see my ex on the dance floor, parading around with her new fitness instructor whose eyes are glued to her chest.

I switch my glance over to my daughter, a vision in her emerald-green dress, her blond hair framing her face. She glances back a me, and our eyes hold and meet.

With a frown, she looks away again. I wonder what my ex-wife has said about me now. Conversation rises and falls around us.

I lean forward and catch a whiff of floral perfume. "I think you have heard some things, but you just don't want to tell me."

Sophie's smile spreads further. "I thought I was the one with trust issues."

I take another sip of my drink, the taste burning a path down to my throat. "Definitely not. You just don't know how to hide it well. So, what have you heard?"

Sophie shakes her head. "I'm not telling you."

"Not even a little bit?"

"Well, there's the superhero suit you keep pressed and laundered in your office," Sophie says, her lips twitching. "And your affinity for women's skin care products."

I sigh. "The first is obviously completely true. I'm glad we got that out of the way right away."

Sophie nods. "I had a feeling."

"As for the second, there's no denying good taste. Women's products are much better."

Sophie sets her drink down and turns; she's facing me completely.

I let my eyes sweep over her, taking in the long slender neck, the plunging neckline of her lilac gown, and a pair of long legs clad in silver heels.

She is even more beautiful up close and personal. A strange longing stirs within me. Music swells and rises in the background.

"What about body care?"

"I think women's shower gels, shampoos, etc. are all superior products."

Sophie's lips twitch again. "I see. Well then, I think the tabloids have another scandal on their hands."

I lean against the counter and pretend to think. "Yeah, I can see the headline now. Jared Fox, a man with more secrets than body hair."

Sophie chokes on her drink and sputters. I thump her on the back. "Want some water?"

Sophie's eyes water as she clears her throat. "No, I'm okay. Thanks."

I take another long sip of my drink and eye her intently. "Of all the weddings in all the world…"

"You had to walk into mine," Sophie jokes, her blush deepening. "If I had known earlier, I would've been nicer."

I finish my drink and offer her a slow once-over. "I'm glad you didn't know. I meant what I said earlier."

Sophie grips her drink with both hands. "Which part?"

"I like a woman who isn't afraid to speak her mind," I repeat, with a smirk. "And you are definitely that."

Sophie lifts the glass up to her lips and eyes me over the rim. "Shouldn't you be circling the party? Looking for potential business partners or something?"

"So, my son has been talking about me."

Sophie sets her drink down and clears her throat. "He doesn't need to. You're Jared Fox."

"Believe it or not, I'm more comfortable in a conference room than I am hobnobbing at a wedding."

"Me too."

"What do you do?"

"I'm a real estate lawyer," Sophie replies after a brief pause. "I know it's a cliché."

"Why is it a cliché?"

Sophie shrugs and glances down at her drink. "Something about lawyers ending up drinking at the bar alone."

I sink into the seat next to her. "You're not alone."

"Does it count if you're my sister's father-in-law?"

I give her a meaningful look. "That depends on whether or not you only see me as that."

Sophie laughs, and the sound is like music to my ears. "That sounds like a loaded question."

"It's not. I'm a straightforward guy."

Sophie's laughter trails off, and she studies me. "I like that. You are not what I expected, you know."

"Were you expecting me to stand in the corner and talk about stock prices and budget projections?"

Sophie chokes back a laugh. "Something like that."

"Sorry to disappoint."

"You haven't," Sophie replies, after a brief pause. "I just didn't expect to have anything to talk about with a man who owns one of the biggest tech companies in the world."

"First of all, you make me sound a lot more boring than I am. Second, I'm glad you've been looking me up."

Sophie frowns. "I don't think you're boring, and I only know things about you because my dentist likes to keep magazines in his office."

"Sure, whatever reason makes you sleep at night."

Sophie's blush turns darker. "It's true. I'm not looking you up or anything."

"Why not?"

Sophie pauses and runs a hand over her face. "Why would I? I don't work in the same field."

"Your interests could be personal."

Sophie's lips lift into a half smile. "Why would they be? I don't know you."

I move closer, catching another whiff of her perfume. "We did share a cab together. There's a lot you can tell about a person when you share a cab ride."

Sophie raises an arched brow. "Like what?"

"Like the fact that you are risk averse, and you like to know what you're getting yourself into before you get into it."

Surprise flickers across Sophie's face. A moment later, she stomps it out. "That was a lucky guess."

"It's an educated guess," I reply, with a wink. "Come on, don't tell me you're not even the least bit impressed."

Sophie hides her smile behind her glass. She takes a few sips, her eyes never leaving my face, and the roar in my ears continues. "So, what if I am?"

"Then I'd have to tell you that you clean up well. I can't decide if you're even more beautiful having just gotten off a plane, covered in sweat, or in your maid of honor's dress."

Sophie rolls her eyes. "Oh, come on. You and I both know you're just trying to butter me up."

I take a long sip of my drink. "Why would I want to do that?"

It's been a while since I've engaged in a conversation like this.

The kind where I don't know where it's going or how it's going to end. It's a breath of fresh air, and suddenly I don't even mind that we're earning a few whispers from people, and a few disapproving looks.

All I care about is the gorgeous woman sitting across from me, acting like I'm the most interesting man in the world.

The feeling is exhilarating, especially because she isn't throwing herself at me.

"I don't know. Maybe you're afraid I'll sue you for emotional damage."

I lift up an eyebrow. "For stealing your cab? That sounds like a lot of unnecessary paperwork. You sure you want to put yourself through that?"

"It's a very serious thing, you know."

"Of course."

Sophie smiles and laughs. "Okay, fine, so I won't sue you for that, but I bet I could find another way and win."

I reach across the table and brush my hand against hers. "Sophie Davenport, you are not what I expected either."

In fact, she is a hell of a lot more than I bargained for. It is one thing for me to flirt with her on the way to the same hotel.

It's another thing entirely for me to envision what her toned and slim body looked like without her dress on.

And the longer I sit there, sipping on my drink and letting the music wash over me, the harder it is for me to remember why I haven't ushered her out of here and into a car.

My reaction to her is visceral and immediate. And I can tell, by the way she's leaning towards me and hanging on my every word, that she feels the same. It makes me want her even more.

A part of me is reluctant to remove my hand, knowing that if I did the spell would break, and real life would come crashing down around both of us.

The other part of me can't bring myself to care that she looks to be half my age, and my son's sister-in law to boot.

None of that seems to matter whenever I look at her. Especially when she brushes her hand against mine, sending a jolt of electricity up my arm. Goddamn it.

I can't even remember the last time a woman had such a primal effect on me. And it's making me want to do all kinds of things to her. Things I shouldn't be thinking of.

Chapter Three: Sophie

Jared leans forward, and he smells like old spice and sandalwood. "Looks like things are winding down. Do you want to get out of here?"

I blow out a breath. "I shouldn't."

As attractive as he is, an even more alluring sight in his pressed suit, with his hair slicked back and a few buttons undone on his shirt, he is still Melanie's father-in-law.

Yet, when he looks at me, his hazel almond shaped eyes seem to see right through me.

And all I can think about is how much I want to run my fingers through his silky hair. Being around him sends all reason right out the window.

For the life of me, I don't understand it.

Jared sits up straighter and flashes me another look that sends a shiver racing up my spine. "Why not? We're both consenting adults here."

He makes a good point, and the longer I stay in his company, the harder it is to resist him. With a sigh, I stand up and nod.

In silence, Jared leads me out of my parents' backyard and onto the quiet moonlight street. My heart is hammering against my chest when a sleek black car pulls up next to the curb.

A uniformed driver holds the door open, and Jared gestures to me. I hesitate before sliding in. Jared is following me and pulling the door shut behind him.

As soon as we peel away from the curb, the driver hits a button, and a partition rises up between us. "Something tells me you do this sort of thing often."

Jared pours me a glass of champagne. "Not as often as you'd think."

Sweat forms on the back of my neck. "Is that so?"

Jared takes a sip from his own glass and inches closer. He pauses to tug on his tie, leaving it askew around his neck. "You're fucking gorgeous, Sophie. And I want you. I'm not going to lie about that."

Another jolt of desire races through me. "I want you too."

Jared takes both of our glasses and sets them down. "So, what are you waiting for?"

Without waiting for a response, he pulls me to him, so I am straddling him, one leg thrown up on either side of him.

He makes a low noise in the back of his throat and digs his nails into my waist. I can feel every inch of him through the fabric of his suit, and it's making me feel light-headed and powerful.

I want to see more of him. My breath hitches in my throat as I fumble with the buttons of his shirt, flicking a few to reveal a smattering of dark chest hair. "Oh."

Jared's mouth spreads into a slow smile. "Like what you see?"

"I do."

Jared's fingers move to my dress, and he hoists it up until it reaches my waist. "I can think of something better."

He cups the back of my neck, and his mouth is feather light and soft against mine. I make a low whimpering noise and melt against him, wave after wave of desire rising through me.

His grip on the back of my neck tightens as I angle my head. I taste champagne and mint on his tongue, a heady mixture that leaves me breathless with anticipation.

Jared rubs himself against me, and I dig my hands into his shoulders. Holy fuck.

I have never felt such an intense attraction before. Like I'm about to explode into a million pieces.

He wrenches his lips away and begins to pepper my neck with hot, open-mouthed kisses. I grip the back of his neck and throw my head back.

His hot breath is on my jaw and on my chest, searing against my flushed skin. I buck against him, and he makes a low growling noise that reverberates inside of my head.

Jared keeps one hand on the small of my waist, and the other lightly grazes my breasts, over the thin fabric of my dress. He sends another jolt of red, hot desire straight to my stomach. I am panting.

The zipper is halfway to my back when I realize the car has come to a stop, and someone is clearing their throat.

I bury my face in the crook of his neck and exhale. "We're here."

Jared draws back to look at me, raw hunger written all over his face. "Let's go."

He peels off his jacket as I climb off him.

In silence, he hands me his jacket, and I drape it over my back. Jared pauses to push the door open and spills outside.

A warm blast of air hits me in the face as he turns and holds his hand out. I stumble out of the car and lose my balance. Jared's eyes don't leave my face as he drapes an arm over my shoulders and leads me up the flight of stairs.

I can't believe I'm doing this.

Half of me wants to run back to my own room and stay there for the rest of the night. The other half of me marvels at the feel of his smooth skin against mine, doing strange things to my insides.

Once we reach the top of the stairs, we step in through the revolving doors, and Jared's thumb begins to trace circles along the inside of my wrist.

Together, we step out into the carpeted lobby, with a glistening chandelier in the center and a group of uniformed men and women standing at attention.

Jared steers me in the direction of the elevator. "What do you feel like eating?"

"Eating?"

Jared hits the button for the elevator and gives me a heated look. "After."

I swallow. "What do you recommend?"

The elevator doors ping open, and I step in. As soon as the doors are closed, Jared pins me against the wall and kisses me again.

This time it's different, it's impatient and demanding, and it leaves every last inch of me buzzing and reeling at his touch.

Jared knows exactly how to kiss a woman. I shouldn't be surprised. He rubs his hands up and down my arms, sending goosebumps up and down my flesh.

I link my fingers over his neck and toss my head to the side. His mouth is demanding, and it drives away all common sense. And every last doubt that I have.

Suddenly, the elevator doors ping open, and Jared peels himself away. He gives me a heated look and links his fingers through mine. I can barely hear past the pounding of my ears as he leads me down another carpeted hallway, with bland gray walls on either side of us.

At the end of the hallway, he stops, takes a card out of his pocket and swipes it.

I catch a brief glimpse of a couch overlooking a large TV, a marble counter in the center of the room, and a large tub in the tile bathroom.

Jared is kicking the door shut with the back of his leg and reaching for me. I hoist myself up and wrap my legs around his waist. He smiles into my skin and carries me into the room, pausing to lower me onto the king-sized bed.

When he steps back to look at me, I see his fingers move to the buttons of his shirt. He undoes one after the other in quick succession, offering me a generous view of his smooth, tanned skin.

My mouth turns dry as I scramble off the bed and wrestle with the zipper on my back. Jared is pushing down his trousers when I manage to get my zipper halfway through.

Wordlessly, he covers the distance between us and spins me around.

My bare back is pressed against him, and it makes the butterflies in my stomach explode.

His fingers are feather light and sure as he pushes the zipper down, so the dress descends to the floor. With a growl, he pushes my hair forward and kisses the back of my neck.

The gesture is intimate and familiar. Like we've done it a million times before.

The response is instant, my entire body humming and coming alive underneath his touch. Jared continues to pepper my back with kisses till he reaches my waist.

Without warning, he spins me around and kneels in front of me. His molten eyes don't leave my face as he takes my panties between his teeth and slides them down.

I have never been more turned on in my entire life.

I want to kiss him again.

I want to feel his mouth on every inch of my skin.

And I want him to bury himself in me, so far in that we can't tell where one begins and the other ends.

Jared lets the panties fall to the floor, and he rises back up to his feet. "You're fucking beautiful, Sophie. You should see what I'm seeing."

"I like the view from where I stand," I whisper, another smattering of goosebumps breaking out across from my flash. "What are you waiting for?"

Jared chuckles and undoes the clasp of my bra.

Once my breasts spill forward, he rubs them together, pinching and flicking the nipples as he does. I release a deep, uneven breath and fall forward against him.

I bring my head to rest against his chest and run my hands up and down the slope of his back, pausing at his waist. Jared lowers his head and takes one nipple between his teeth, sending a jolt through me.

As soon as he moves to the other breast, my vision turns white, and I buck against him.

He pushes me back onto the bed, and I am falling, unable to see or hear or breath anything else. Jared is everywhere all at once, invading my senses and making me forget why he and I shouldn't be together in the first place.

None of those reasons matter.

Not when Jared kisses me like he's been starving for air.

Not when I link my fingers over his waist and draw him closer.

And not when he positions himself at my entrance and thrusts.

Jared fills every last inch of me and draws back to look at me, but I can't decipher the look on his face.

All I see is hunger and yearning, the kind I am sure is mirrored in my own eyes. His eyes stay on my face as he drops a hand between us and rubs my sensitive bundle of nerves. I moan and squeeze my eyes shut.

His growls and pants reverberate inside of my head. Before I know it, I am bucking and writhing underneath him, the force of my pleasure ripping through me.

Jared eases out and slams back into me, eliciting a low, throaty whimper. He brings his head to rest against the headboard and his rhythm changes.

All at once, he is thrusting in and out of me with wild, and animal-like abandon.

The kind that leaves me breathless and clawing at his back. It still isn't enough.

I need more of him, of his skin on mine, of his hot breath inches away from my ear.

And of the vulnerability and emotion coursing through me. I feel like I am invincible like I'm on the edge of something great.

Jared dips his head and presses his mouth to mine. Every stroke, every touch, every kiss has me more and more addicted to him. Until I am falling again, gasping and chanting his name as I do.

His own release follows soon after, and Jared's entire body shakes. He is slick with sweat and gasping for breath by the time he's done.

With an exhale, he rolls off of me and collapses onto the mattress. I stare up at the ceiling and place a hand on my chest over the thundering of my heart.

Holy shit. Did I really just sleep with my sister's father-in-law? And why the hell do I want to do it again?

Chapter Four: Jared

"Are you sure I look okay?"

I lower my phone and glance up at her, a vision in her silk red dress with a plunging neckline.

Her hair is in an updo and her black heels are clicking against the floor. Slowly, I stand up, pocket my phone and lift the drink up to my lips.

Goddamn. Sophie looks even better in the dress than I imagined. I have a brief image of myself pushing the dress up to her waist and carrying her back into the bedroom.

I see her sprawled on the bed, her hair fanned out behind her and a hungry look in her eyes.

When I blink, Sophie has inched closer, the floral scent of her perfume making my stomach give an odd little dip. She is breathtaking.

I still can't understand the effect she has on me, even though it's been two weeks of getting to know every inch of her. In more ways than one.

Sophie Davenport is a surprising woman.

Sophie's blood red lips curl into a smile as she waves a hand in front of my face. "Hello? Why do you have that look on your face? Does it look that bad?"

I finish off my drink, the liquid burning a path down my throat. "You look amazing, Sophie. That dress looks so much better on you than it did on the mannequin."

"It's one of the nicest dresses I've ever owned," Sophie murmurs, flush stealing across her cheeks. "Thank you, but you know you didn't have to."

"I wanted to." I button up my jacket and hold an arm out to her. "No one is going to be able to look away tonight."

Sophie stands up straighter. "I already feel like I don't fit in."

"It's a charity event. You'll enjoy it, I promise." I press a kiss on her cheek and pat her hand. "Shall we?"

Sophie slips her hand into the crook of my elbow and smiles. "We shall."

In silence, I lead her out of the apartment and into the elevator. She inches closer and brings her head to rest in the crook of my neck.

I press a kiss to the side of her head, the butterflies in my stomach doing somersaults. When the elevator doors ping open, we move down the lobby, and toward the uniformed doorman, who tilts his head in our direction.

Outside, my black car is waiting by the curb, the driver already holding the door open.

I pause to help Sophie scoop up her dress and wait until she adjusts the folds around her.

Once she's settled, I climb in behind her and reach for her hand. She spends the entire ride glancing out the window and fidgeting.

We pull up outside the hotel, catching sight of the two marble columns out front, and enter to find a large set of stairs leading to French double doors.

She is gawking. She twists her head to face me, and I chuckle at the wonder and awe written on her face.

I like spoiling Sophie already. And I can't wait to walk into the room and be the envy of every man there.

I press a kiss on her wrist and push the door open. Out of the corner of my eye, I see a flash of movement, and a group of well-dressed men and women wave at me.

I give them a small smile and nod before holding my hand out.

Sophie's heel-clad feet emerge first, followed by the rest of her. When she straightens her back and tucks her arm into mine, I am dumbstruck all over again.

She glides next to me, earning a few curious glances from the people around her.

At the double doors, she glances over at me. I see the hint of a smile on her lips. The doors are pushed open, and we step inside, underneath a glittering chandelier.

A spacious ballroom reveals several tables set up on either side, populated by uniformed waiters with canapés.

A small podium with a poster of a child on it is the main attraction. Next to me, Sophie is taking it all in, a myriad of emotions dancing across her face.

I take two glasses of champagne off of a passing tray and hand her one. "Here's to us."

Sophie lifts the glass up to her lips. "Isn't it a little premature to be drinking to that?"

I shake my head and take a sip. "I disagree. I think it's exactly the right time. We've got the world at our feet, Sophie. There's so much I want to show you."

And even more than that I want to experience with her.

For the rest of the night, Sophie is hanging on my arm as I circle the room, introducing her with a smile in every circle.

She handles all of the attention and curiosity well, keeping her head held high and a smile on her face.

By the time we are shown to our table, my feelings for her have grown even more.

I place a hand on her knee during the event. She takes my free hand and laces her fingers through mine.

By the end of the night, I have not heard a single word and all I can think about is taking Sophie back to the apartment.

After saying our goodbyes, I usher her into the car, lift the partition, and draw her to me.

Her mouth is hot and sweet against mine. I am addicted, and I can't get enough.

When we reach the apartment, we barely make it out of the car without ripping each other's clothes off.

Hours later, exhausted and spent, she curls up against me and drifts off to sleep.

In the morning, when the early morning sun pours in, tiny particles of light dancing on the floor, I sit up and rub a hand over my face.

I glance over at Sophie's sleeping form, her hair tousled around her face, and her expression serene. She stirs when I slid back onto the mattress and twist onto my side.

Sophie opens one eye, so she's looking directly at me, and my stomach gives an odd little dip. "Good morning."

"It is now." I press a kiss to her lips and lean back. "How did you sleep?"

"Like a log," Sophie replies, in a thick voice. "How long have you been up?"

"I just got up a few minutes ago, and isn't the expression like a baby?"

Sophie snorts. "I've got cousins. I know for a fact that babies rarely sleep. We need to retire that expression."

"Yes, ma'am. Any other requests?"

Sophie's other eye opens, and she gives me a sleepy smile. "Breakfast?"

"How would you feel about eggs and pancakes?"

Sophie flips onto her side and draws the covers up to her chin. "I think I would love that, but I shouldn't eat that much first thing in the morning."

"You're going to need your energy," I tell her, with a smirk. "Trust me on this."

Sophie giggles and sits up, letting the sheets fall onto the bed. "In that case, how would you feel about a shower?"

"It's like you can read my mind."

·♥·♥·♥·♥·♥·

"I thought it was hilarious," I whisper into her ear, pausing to press a kiss to her cheek. "You shouldn't worry so much about what people think."

Sophie shrugs and looks up at me. "I can't help it. You know that I'm a people pleaser."

We stop at our table, and I pull out Sophie's chair before sitting down.

Around us, the other guests in the restaurant are doing the same, floating from one table to the other, while the waiters and waitresses move about effortlessly in a choregraphed dance they have done hundreds of times.

I can't help but feel like Sophie belongs in this world of fancy parties and glittering ballrooms.

As far as I'm concerned, she fits right in, and I don't care what anyone else thinks.

Granted, I've had more than a few of my acquaintances express their concern, especially after learning her age, but I'm not going to give any of them the time of the day.

They have no idea how I feel about Sophie. Like I'm young and full of hope again.

In the past few weeks alone, she's made me feel like a brand-new man. And a part of me doesn't even care that we're moving fast.

I want her in every single part of my life. It's why I take her out to as many parties and events as I can.

"You have absolutely nothing to worry about," I repeat, with a smile. "Once they get to know you, they'll see what I see."

"And what about when they get to know you?"

I chuckle and squeeze her hand. "Thankfully, they haven't been able to see behind the mask yet."

Sophie sets down her glass of water and looks over at me. "You know, I think they'd love it if they got to know the real Jared. The one who likes to stay in his pajamas until noon, doing crosswords and yoga."

"Stop ruining my reputation," I tease, pausing to reach for my glass of water. "Next thing you know, you'll be telling them that I like playing video games."

Sophie giggles. "That one is our little secret."

I take a long sip of my water and turn my chair, so I'm facing her. "Tell me something I don't know."

"That could take some time." Sophie picks up the napkin and sets it down on her lap. "And I don't think your friends will appreciate me taking up all your time."

I wave her comment away. "They'll get over it. So, tell me."

Sophie's expression turns thoughtful. "I want to buy my own island someday, fill it with people I like and get away from the world."

"I like the sound of that. Do I get to live on this island with you?"

Sophie's lips lift into a half smile. "If you play your cards right."

I lean forward, and her breath hitches in her throat. "What if I promise to be really, really nice?"

"I'll think about it." Sophie playfully shoves me away, her cheeks turning a bright red. "It's your turn to tell me a secret."

"I'm not wearing any underwear."

Sophie chokes on her water, earning a few looks from the other restaurant goers.

When she regains her color, she pinches me underneath the table. "You're not supposed to tell me that kind of secret."

I shrug. "You didn't specify what kind."

Sophie sputters and shakes her head. "Obviously, I didn't mean that kind. We're at a restaurant. We've got to keep it PG thirteen or something."

My hand darts underneath the table and grazes her knee, on display underneath her skirt. "Or we could find a closet somewhere and have some fun."

Sophie laughs. "I'm being serious."

"So am I."

She gives me a pointed look and waits.

I draw my hand away and exhale. "Fine. When I was younger, I wanted to be a detective."

"Like Sherlock Holmes?"

"More like Shaggy Rogers."

"Shaggy Rogers from Scooby Doo?"

I nod and smile at the waiter who brings us our bowls of soup. "The one and only."

Sophie tilts her head to the side and studies me. "Yeah, I could see you pulling off a goatee and being stoned most of the time."

I pause with the spoon halfway to my lips. "I feel like I should be offended."

"It's a compliment."

I push my chair closer to hers and drape an arm over her shoulders. "Here's another secret. Right now, with you, there's nowhere else I'd rather be."

Sophie blushes and kisses my cheek. "There's nowhere else I'd rather be either."

Chapter Five: Sophie

"And did you see what she was wearing? It's so obvious that he's the one buying all her clothes. She looks washed out and like she's trying too hard."

"And did you see the way she held her spoon? Could it be any more obvious that she doesn't know how to handle herself?"

"I do not know what Jared sees in her."

A smattering of giggles rises up, filling my stomach with acid. I remove my head from the stall door and push it open.

Once I step out, three pairs of eyes look up and gawk at me. With my head held high, I walk over to the sink and switch on the faucet.

My heart is hammering against my chest as I lather my hands with soap and run them underneath the warm water.

I feel their eyes on me the entire time, sizing me up. It makes me want to run out of the bathroom and hide somewhere.

Instead, I finish washing my hands and dry them on a paper towel. As soon as I walk out of the bathroom, I hear them break out into laughter.

The knot in my stomach tightens. While a part of me knows that winning over Jared's social circle isn't going to be easy, I didn't expect them to be so cruel. And judgmental.

Everything from the way they stare at me to the backhanded comments made while I stand a few feet away.

It takes every ounce of self-control I had to stand there and take it all in stride. All because of Jared. If it hadn't been for him, I would've already walked away.

But I can't, not when I know that I'm in too deep with him.

"There you are." Jared materializes in his suit, sporting an easy smile. He hands me a glass of champagne and tucks my arm into his elbow. "I know McGuire's stories are boring, but you don't have to hide in the bathroom to avoid them."

I swallow. "I wasn't."

Jared stops in the middle of the crowded hotel ballroom and twists to face me, his entire face etched in concern. "What's wrong?"

I clear my throat. "I overheard some of the wives and girlfriends talking about me...."

Jared's brows furrow together. "Whatever they said, it's only because they're jealous. You are smart, funny, sexy. You're also driven, ambitious and dedicated.

Trust me, they wish they could be half the woman you are."

I tilt my head to the side and study him. "You do know it's not that simple, right?"

Jared shrugs and lifts the glass up to his lips. "It is to me."

I sigh. "Maybe we should just go home."

Jared lowers his glass and reaches for my hand. "Okay, how about this? How about we stay for one more hour? There's still some people I want to talk to. Then we can go."

I nod. "Okay."

Jared finishes off his drink and flashes me a smile.

The butterflies in my stomach erupt into a frenzy, and I offer him a small smile.

Out of the corner of my eye, I see a flash of movement, and women appear from the bathroom, all wearing expensive dresses, and their perfectly coiffed hair piled on top of their head. When they see me, they bend their heads together and begin to whisper.

I straighten my back and turn away from them. "Okay, let's go schmooze."

"That's the spirit." Jared gives me a quick wink and steps forward. "Don't worry about those women. They've got nothing on you."

Except it isn't just the women. Although I appreciate Jared's optimism, and his attempts to gloss everything over, it is clear that most of the people in this room don't think I belong there. And it isn't just the people at the corporate dinner.

Every time Jared and I step out together, rumors and whispers seem to follow. Everything from the way I dress to the way I speak is being put under the microscope.

As a lawyer, I am used to a certain level of scrutiny, particularly in court, but this is nothing at all like that.

Beneath their rehearsed smiles and their glazed looks was a sharpness and single-mindedness that left me with a bad taste in the back of my mouth.

At the end of every night, I am usually all too relieved to curl up next to Jared in the back of the car and stroke his arm.

He still can't see any of it. As far as he's concerned, being on his arm is enough.

I wish it was that simple, Jared. You and I both know it isn't. Especially because the age difference is the least of our problems.

Over the past few weeks, I have been trying to find the courage to come clean to Melanie.

The problem is that every time I pick up the phone, and we get to talking, I panic and keep replaying what it's like to be in the same room with Jared's social circle.

I imagine my sister having the same kind of horrified and angry reaction.

And a part of me isn't sure she'd be in the wrong. Jared was, after all, still her father-in-law, a man who is twice my age, and the owner of one of the biggest multi-billion-dollar corporations in the world.

I know what the optics look like, and I know what people are thinking of me, but I can't seem to help myself.

I'm just glad Mel's and Cameron's social circles are not the same as Jared's. This gives me the time and option to take my time in telling them about my relationship with Jared.

I like being around Jared, and how he makes me feel like I'm the only woman in the world. And I know I'm falling hard and fast.

Jesus. How did I get myself into this mess?

With a slight shake of my head, I allow Jared to steer me toward the next group of people, older men and women with salt and pepper hair who look right through me.

During the conversation, they acknowledge me once, wrinkle up their noses at the fact that I am a lawyer and move on. I spend the rest of the night with lead in my stomach.

At the end of the hour, Jared makes his excuses, and we step out into the brisk night air.

He peels off his jacket, drapes it over my shoulders and laces his fingers through mine. At the bottom of the stairs, he pauses to press a kiss on my cheek. He helps me get into the car.

Once settled in the back, I bring my head to rest against his shoulders and sigh.

When we reach his apartment, all traces of my earlier good mood are gone. And all I can think about is the endless parade of parties and events where I'm judged.

The uniformed doorman smiles and holds the door open for us. Jared tilted his head in the man's direction, and his grip on my hand tightens.

In the elevator, I slip out of my heels and curl into his side. Being near Jared is comforting, but it does nothing to help ward off the unease.

Once the elevator doors ping open, Jared and I step forward. He unlocks the door to his apartment and waits for me to go in. He kicks the door shut behind him and presses a kiss on my forehead.

He kisses me with such tenderness and emotion that it takes my breath away.

"I'm going to go take a shower," Jared announces, pausing to tug on his tie. "Join me?"

"Maybe later. I should call Melanie back. She's tried to get in touch a few times."

Jared nods and flicks open a few buttons. "Okay. We should order something to eat. The food at the event was shit."

I give him a half smile. "Sure."

He rounds the corner, and a few moments later, I hear the water running. Suddenly tears start to run down my face.

That heavy feeling has to find its way out somehow, tears sound good right now. After a few minutes of letting my heavy and sad emotions to roll down my cheeks, I feel a bit better.

Then I let the heels fall to the floor with a clutter and lift up my purse. With a frown, I run a hand over my face, clear my throat and press my phone to my ear.

It rings a few times before Melanie picks up, sounding breathless and confused.

"Hey, sis. What's up?"

"Sorry, I missed your call earlier. I was getting ready for this event."

"You've been going to a lot of those lately. This have anything to do with that mystery man you've been dating?"

I blow out a breath. "Yeah."

"You know you don't have to hide him from us, right? I know mom was riding you pretty hard about getting married next, but I can keep her off your back."

"Thanks, Mel."

"What's wrong? What happened?"

"Nothing is wrong."

Melanie sighs. "Soph, I've known you my whole life. I know when something is wrong. Did you and your date get into a fight or something?"

"No, things are going really well actually."

"You don't sound happy about that."

"It's these people he associates with. His social circle, I mean," I whisper, with a quick look over my shoulders. "They're awful, Mel. I am trying to ignore them and their comments, but they make it so hard."

Melanie's voice drifts off, and I hear a muffled voice in the background. A door opens and closes, and her voice comes back on, clearer than before. "What did they do?"

"I don't know if I know how to explain it." I lower myself onto the couch and prop my feet up on the table, the folds of my dress rustling around me. "It's like you know when you're dreaming, and you have this feeling that you're not supposed to be there. And you realize it's because you're back in your high school classroom, or you're naked in the middle of a football field during a big game?"

"I'm confused. So, you think they're judging you, or you think that you don't belong?"

I stare up at the ceiling and twirl a lock of hair between my fingers. "Both. I already told you that this guy I'm dating is rich, and from a completely different world...I mean, you know me. My idea of fancy is using a napkin when I eat takeout."

"Is he the one who's making you feel like you're not enough?"

I lower my legs and sit up straighter. "No, not at all. I like being with him, Mel. He makes me laugh, and he's smart and considerate. And when I'm with him, nothing else matters."

"Someone's got it bad," Melanie teases, in a singsong voice. "Now, I definitely have to meet him."

"I don't know, Mel. It feels like we're on borrowed time here. I don't think these people are ever going to accept me, not when they think I'm beneath them."

"Soph, listen to me, I can't even remember the last time I heard you talk about a guy like this. You can't let those idiots get to you, okay? You deserve to be happy, and if he makes you happy, nothing else matters."

I sigh. "What if they never accept me?"

How am I supposed to survive in Jared's world if everyone plays by a different set of rules?

"Then they can go screw themselves. Look, I know how you like to play things safe, and you don't like unnecessary risks, but I think this is worth it, Soph."

I ran a hand over my face. "How do you know?"

"Because I'm your sister, and I know stuff," Melanie replies, a smile in her voice. "And I know that you'll tell me about this guy when you're ready. In the meantime, take your little sister's advice. You'll thank me for it."

Another voice rose in the background, and Melanie's voice is muffled.

"Oh, by the way, did I tell you that my father-in-law is dating a younger woman? Cameron is pissed."

My heart sputters and crashes. "Why?"

"He's pretty sure she's just using his dad. He's probably not wrong. Why else would a woman half his age date him?"

I swallow past the lump in my throat. "Right, I've got to go. Takeout is here. Talk later?"

"Okay, love you."

I stand up and clutch the phone to my ear. "Love you too."

Right there I decide not to tell Melanie about Jared, at least not now.

Chapter Six: Jared

"Do you give up yet?"

Sophie leaps over the bed and holds her arms up on either side of her. "Never. I'll never surrender."

"Never is a really long time," I remind her, with a smile. "Wouldn't it just be easier to give up? There's ice cream in it for you."

Sophie scowls. "Stop trying to butter me up. I see what you're trying to do."

I circle the bed and approach her. "I'm not trying to do anything, Soph. Come on, give me some credit."

Sophie shrieks and darts away. "Stop it. I don't want to be tickled."

"You know the rules of the bet, and you lost. So, now you have to take it like an adult."

Sophie sticks her tongue out at me and dances away. "Says who?"

I throw myself at her and chuckle. "Says me."

"Who made you the boss?"

We fall sideways onto the bed, and I pin her underneath me. "Well, I am the boss."

Sophie wriggles and bucks against me. "You're not the boss of me."

I give her a slow, wicked smile. "No, but I could be"

Sophie rolls her eyes. "We're not even in the same field of work. You own a tech company, and I'm a real estate lawyer."

"So? I'm always looking for good people to hire. And I think you'd look great in a tight little skirt and high heels."

Sophie's face turns bright red. "It sounds like you want me to come work for you, so you can live out a fantasy."

I lift her arms up over her head and dip my head, so I'm inches away from her mouth. "Guilty as charged."

"Motion to dismiss," Sophie says, breathlessly.

I move my mouth closer to hers, and she stops squirming. "On what grounds?"

"On the grounds that you are badgering me."

I chuckle. "I don't think that would hold up in court."

Sophie laughs, the sound like music to my ears. "It's a good thing we're not in court."

"Yeah, it's a shame. I'd let you take me down in court any day."

Sophie scoffs and looks directly into my eyes. "I'd take you down on my own merit, Foxy. Court is my playground. You won't know what hit you."

I shift and move away from her. "Is that so?"

"Absolutely."

She shifts and maneuvers, and I get off of her. Then she's pushing me onto the bed and straddling me.

My eyes widen in surprise as she lowers herself onto me, her nightshirt riding further up her thighs.

I lower my hands to her waist and squeeze. She swats my hands away and shakes a finger at me.

"My court, my rules, remember?"

I smirk and lift my hands up. "Okay, where do you want me to put my hands, counsel?"

"Over your head," Sophie instructs, in a thick voice. "And don't move unless I tell you."

"You're so bossy," I tell her, with another smirk. "It's fucking hot."

"Sucking up to counsel won't get you anywhere."

I reach between us and fondle her over her shirt. "How about now?"

Sophie's mouth parts, and a thin sheen of sweat breaks out over her forehead. "I know what you're trying to do, and it's not going to work."

I squeeze her breasts and shrug. "I'm not trying to do anything. I'm just expressing admiration. Counsel has an impressive body of work."

Sophie chokes back a laugh, her face turning even more red. "I'm onto you, Foxy."

"And all over me," I add, flashing her a wink. "I'm completely at your mercy."

Sophie sighs and lowers her head. I lift a leg up, and she loses her balance, causing her to pitch forward.

I cup the back of her neck, lift my head to it and capture her lips with mine. She sighs and melts into the kiss, tasting delicious.

I can't get enough of her. Every cell in my body yearns for her. For her touch, for her body against mine, and her mouth soft and yielding where mine is demanding and unapologetic.

A swell of emotion rises within my chest, and my heart is pounding in my ears.

Before I can deepen the kiss, the shrill ringing of a phone interrupts. Sophie wrenches her lips away, bright eyes glazed with hunger.

She glances over at the nightstand, a furrow appearing between her brows.

I latch onto her neck, licking and nipping the sensitive skin there. She throws her head back and makes a low whimpering noise.

"Just ignore it," I whisper, in between kisses. "Whoever it is, you can call them back."

"It could be one of my important clients," Sophie says, uncertain. She shudders when I sit up and push her hair over her shoulders. "I should probably get it."

"Don't mind me," I reply, pausing to give her a long look. In one quick move, I snatch her phone off the table and hand it to her.

She presses it to her ear and murmurs as I rub myself against her. Her eyes widen when I drop my head on top of her chest.

When I begin rubbing my stubble over the thin fabric of her shirt, her voice goes breathy.

"Yes, we can look into it on Monday," Sophie responds, in a strained voice. "No, I don't think that should be an issue."

I smile and sink my teeth into her flesh.

Sophie bites back a moan. "Mr. Montrose, I don't want you to worry about any of that. You're in good hands."

I palm her over her shirt and wriggle my hips. "So are you."

Sophie's breath catches in her throat. "Mr. Montrose, I'm with a client right now. I'm going to have to call you back."

As soon as the call ends, I flip her onto her back and kiss her soundly.

When I draw back, she has a dazed expression on her face. "You make a solid point."

I pin her arms over her head and smile. "See? I told you that you'd see things my way eventually."

"I really have to attend to this client," Sophie whispers in my ear as she pushes me off playfully.

· ♥ · ♥ · ♥ · ♥ · ♥ ·

I kiss the back of her neck and set the mug down in front of her. "You sure you don't want to take a break?"

Sophie glances up, removes her glasses and rubs her face. "I can't. I wasn't lying earlier about it being a big client. He's also a big headache."

The other chair makes a low screeching sound as I slide it across the terrace.

I set it down across from her, sit down and reach for her feet. "Is there anything I can do to help?"

Sophie puts her glasses back on and rolls her shoulders. "Nah, I just need to figure out a way to be everywhere all at once."

"At least we got lucky that we live in the same city," I remind her.

I rub the soles of her feet. "If anyone can figure it out, I'm sure it'll be you."

Sophie sighs and sinks lower into her seat. "You have a lot of faith in me."

"I've seen you when you set your mind to something. That sink the other day didn't stand a chance."

Sophie smiles, and her entire face lights up. "It didn't, did it?"

"I've never seen a woman who is so handy with tools. What other surprises are you hiding from me, Davenport? Are you some kind of spy?"

"We've retired the term," Sophie says, her lips twitching. "We prefer the term information seekers now."

"That's a mouthful. I like spy better."

"I'll make a note of that to the agency." Wisps of her hair escape from her bun and frame her face, giving her a youthful and more vulnerable look. "I'm not as handy as you think. I just had to do a lot of stuff on my own."

"Because your dad wasn't around as often?"

Sophie leans forward and sets her laptop down on the coffee table.

She looks right at home on my lawn chair in the middle of my terrace, with the afternoon sun over her head.

"Yeah, exactly. I know it was a long time ago, when dad's job was very demanding, he missed a lot of family events."

I reach for her other foot and apply pressure. "Because you were older, you had to learn to do things on your own. Melanie probably doesn't remember it as well."

Sophie tilts her head up to the sun. "Dad eventually changed his job and he was more at home and involved when we got older."

"You're a good sister. Your parents seem to be doing well together now."

Sophie snorts and glances over at me. "Yeah, I don't feel like such a good sister. Melanie is going to kill me when she finds out about this. To be honest, they never had any issues, he was working most of the time providing for us."

"Cameron will probably kill me too."

Sophie's expression turns sad. "I know we said we'd tell them because we have nothing to hide...but every time I think about it, my skin breaks out into a rash."

"We'll both tell them when they're ready," I reply, after a brief pause. "We're not hiding anything, Soph. We're just getting to know each other."

Sophie's lips lift into a half smile. "It feels like you've gotten to know me pretty well."

I set her feet down and lean forward to give her a kiss. "Good."

Sophie links her fingers over my neck. "About that massage I was promised..."

My hands fall to her waist and squeeze. "Is that what we're calling it now?"

Sophie throws her head back and laughs. "Get your head out of the gutter. I mean an actual massage."

"Sure, sure. Whatever you want to call it."

Sophie playfully shoves me and stands up. "You're insatiable."

"Only for you." I stand up and draw her to me. "You're the only one who can make me feel this way."

Sophie studies my face. "You don't say much about your ex-wife."

"There's nothing much to say. We drifted apart. It happens sometimes."

Sophie frowns. "You were happy at some point, right?"

I nod and take her hand in mine. "Yeah, we were, but we got married young. And we both grew up and turned into different people. I know Violet blames work, but we were drifting apart long before that."

"What about your daughter? Melanie mentioned that you two are estranged."

I lift her hand up to my lips and press a kiss there. "She blames me for the divorce, and she hasn't quite gotten over it yet."

Sophie's expression turns soft. "It's okay."

"Now, if you're done drilling me, how about we go inside, and I can give you that massage?"

"I am not drilling you."

I tug her inside and scoop her up into my arms. "Call it whatever you want. I don't care."

She shrieks and giggles as I carry her into the bedroom and set her down on the bed.

Sophie stands up and stares at me through hooded eyes. She changes out of her clothes, left stark naked in the middle of my bedroom.

Wordlessly, she gives me her back and crawls onto the bed.

With her face pressed into a pillow, she makes a low muffled sound.

I reach for the massage oil on the nightstand, and the bed dips underneath my weight. "This is a good look on you."

"You're not going to convince me to go outside naked."

"I had to try." I press a kiss to the center of her shoulder blades and smile.

When I'm done, Sophie flips onto her side and watches me. "Thank you."

"I know it's hard for me to talk about my ex," I whisper, pausing to tuck a lock of hair behind her ear. "She's my past, Soph. You have nothing to worry about because I'm crazy about you."

Her lips spread into a slow and shy smile. "I'm crazy about you too, Jared."

Chapter Seven: Sophie

"Why is my suitcase here?"

"I packed it for you," Jared says, pausing to poke his head out of the bathroom. He takes the toothbrush out of his mouth and flashes me a smile. "I figured it was time to celebrate."

I perch on the edge of the bed and bring one leg up over the other. "What are we celebrating?"

"You won one of the biggest cases in your career." Jared's voice drifts over to me, muffled and unclear.

"It's a pretty big deal, Soph. You should be proud of yourself."

"I am proud of myself."

Jared steps back into the room in a pair of shorts and a T-shirt. "Good because I'm proud of you too. "

I look up at him and raise an eyebrow. "You still haven't explained the suitcase."

"We're going on a trip," Jared tells me, with a smile. "I got you some new clothes for the occasion."

"I don't need new clothes, and most people typically celebrate by going out to dinner."

"Most people don't have a private jet waiting for them," Jared replies, before drawing me to him. He gives me a quick peck and steps away again. "We'd better hurry up. I want to be there by noon."

"By noon? Jared, are you being serious?"

Jared spins around and gives me a smile. "Yeah, why wouldn't I be?"

"Because we can't just pack up and leave?"

Jared gives me another kiss and wheels the bags behind him. "Why not?"

I follow him into the living room. "Because I...do I need my passport? and my stuff...how?"

"I already made sure all of the travel documents have been taken care of," Jared replies, without looking at me. "And you can go over the contents of your bag before we leave."

I huff and let my arms fall to my sides. "Can I at least take a shower?"

"The private lounge at the airport has a shower." Jared leaves the suitcases by the door and turns to face me. "You can shower there if you want."

"I'd rather shower here. I won't take too long." I reach him and give him a kiss. "I'll be right back."

When I emerge out of the shower, steam follows me into the room.

I feel better as I wriggle into a pair of jeans and shirt. I grab my purse and charger and step back into the living room.

Jared is on the terrace, on the phone, the early morning sun slanted behind him. He flashes me a smile through the glass.

I lean against the door and tap my watch. He laughs and shakes his head.

"You're going to make us late," I tell him, as he steps in through the double doors. "Come on, hurry up."

Jared smacks my butt on his way past. "I'm not the one who had to take a shower."

"You wouldn't have liked being forced so sit next to sweaty me after a run."

"I love sweaty you." Jared places his sunglasses on top of his nose and unlocks the door.

In the hallway, he pauses to punch in the security code. He drapes an arm over my shoulders and kisses my cheek. In the elevator, I clasp my hands behind my back and try to ignore the knots in my stomach.

I am nervous about going away with Jared. But I can't deny that it feels right to be with him.

When the car pulls up outside a private runway, I press my face to the glass and gawk at the plane.

In a flurry of movement, we are escorted onto the plane and immediately handed drinks.

A bright eyed, blonde hair flight attendant takes our bags and stows them away.

I am buzzing with excitement the entire time, and it has everything to do with the man sitting across from me.

His phone already pressed to his ear. I lean back in the chair, squeeze my eyes and drift off to sleep.

Sometime later, someone shakes me awake, and my head feels heavy. I rub my hands over my face and force one eye open.

Jared's face swims in and out of focus till I pry my other eye open. I see his smile. He touches his lips to my forehead and holds a hand out.

With a yawn, I take his hand and let him pull me to my feet. "S'happening?"

"We're here," Jared replies, pausing to push my hair out of my eyes. "Your chariot awaits."

I giggle and follow him down the aisle of the plane. As soon as the door opens, we are met with a blast of hot air that makes the hairs on the back of my neck stand up.

A black car is waiting on the runway, and a uniformed driver is gazing at us expectantly. Jared nods to everyone on his way past and whisks me into the car.

I rub my hand over my face again and pause. Outside, the world is rushing past in hues of blue and green.

There is thick foliage on either side of us and crystal blue waters that glisten underneath the sun. The car inches forward steadily.

The road ahead is mostly empty save for a few trucks. I squint into the sun-soaked distance and try to make out any distinguishing features.

"Where are we?"

Jared brings my hand up to his lips. "Take a guess."

I roll the window down and inhale, the smell of spices wafting up my nostrils, followed by the humidity. "Somewhere in Asia?"

Jared chuckles. "That's pretty broad, but yes. We're in Bali."

I whip around to face him, and my stomach gives an odd little churn. "Bali as in Bali, Indonesia?"

Jared leans back against the leather chairs and smiles. "One and the same."

I throw myself at him and hug him tightly. "Jared, you didn't have to do all of this."

"I know Bali has been on your bucket list for years," Jared whispers, into my ear. "I couldn't have wished for a better place."

I stir and draw back to look at him. "You know you don't have to do all of this, right? I'd still like you even if you were broke and eating ramen out of a cup."

"Even though I snore like a bear?"

I giggle and tuck myself into his side. "I can live with that."

"In that case, I'm afraid that I have to tell you something important."

I look up at him, and my brows furrow together. "What is it?"

Jared's expression turns serious, his almond-shaped eyes focused on me intently. "I didn't want to say this when we first dating because I wasn't sure if it was going to affect the future of our relationship."

A hard knot forms in the center of my stomach.

Is this part where he breaks up with me?

Tells me that he discovered we're all wrong for each other?

He couldn't have picked a worse time to do it.

"Tell me."

"The thing is...I hate, and I really do mean hate...sushi."

I sputter and slap him on the arm. "That's what you wanted to tell me? Dang it! Jared. What's the matter with you? You scared the shit out of me."

Jared throws his head back and roars with laughter. "You should've seen the look on your face. You looked so worried."

I slap his arm again and scowl. "Not funny."

"I thought it was hilarious."

"You have an awful sense of humor."

The car screeches to a halt in front of a two-story brick villa with a small garden out front.

Jared pushes the door open and rummages through the mail box. He produces a key and waves it at me.

I smile, get out of the car and folds my arms over my chest.

"I still haven't forgiven you."

Jared unlocks the door and walks over to me. Wordlessly, he crouches and swoops me into his arms. "I'll make it up to you."

I flail and grip his shirt. "Just don't drop me."

Jared steps through the door, his eyes sweeping over the place before they land on me. Slowly, he sets me down on my feet and kisses me.

I sway a little, a smile hovering on my lips. I spin around, taking in the pool overlooking crystal clear waters and a wooden outdoor patio with lawn chairs scattered throughout.

Through the double doors, I see an open kitchen with a marble counter in the center.

There is a cream-colored living room with plush chairs, overlooking a large TV propped over a mantel.

Holy shit. It really is beautiful.

Jared presses himself against my back and wraps his arms around my waist. "What do you think?"

I lose a deep breath. "I think this is the nicest place I've ever seen, but it's so big."

"There's a jacuzzi on the roof."

I spin around to face him and link my fingers over his neck. "Now, you're just showing off."

"I like showing off for you." Jared kisses me and hoists me up. In between giggles, he carries me up the stairs and in the direction of a door that opens to reveal a large bed, a bathroom with a tub, and a balcony overlooking the water.

He sets me down on my feet and makes a sweeping hand gesture.

"This place is ours for a week. I rented out a boat for us."

"Jared, this is really too much."

Jared shakes his head and crosses over to the balcony. He inhales the crisp, ocean air and smiles. "I'm going to go make a few phone calls. Why don't you change, and I'll meet you downstairs?"

I gave him a quick hug on the way past. While I go through my clothes, I take pictures of the room and view, unable to stop myself from sending them to Melanie.

After I change into a black and white one piece and a coverup, I make my way down the stairs.

Jared is leaning against the kitchen counter, afternoon light pouring in behind him and giving him a warm ethereal glow.

The sight of him sends a wave of emotion washing over me. It only intensifies when he looks over at me and smiles. Goddamn, I really am in trouble when it comes to this man.

He ends the call, pulls me to him and kisses me. When he leads me out the back door and down a hidden path, leading onto the beach, I am overwhelmed with emotion.

A small boat is waiting for us on the edge of the water, an older man with a weathered face and streaks of gray hair at the helm.

Jared helps me onto the boat, and we settle in. We spend the next few hours swimming and laughing.

By the time the sun dips below the horizon, my stomach is grumbling in protest, and my mouth hurts from smiling.

I climb onto the boat first and make my way below deck. Jared joins me for a quick shower before disappearing upstairs.

Once I come out, I see the table already set in the middle of the boat, underneath the glow of the moon. My heart sputters and grows to twice its size.

He really did make me feel like the luckiest woman in the world.

Jared holds my chair out for me and waits till I sit down. "I asked the chef to make your favorite."

I reach for a glass of water and take a long sip. "This is all so amazing. It really is. It means so much that you went through all of this effort."

Jared sits across from me, his face bathed in the silver glow of the moon. "I wanted to, Soph."

"I've never met anyone like you," I whisper, over the thundering of my heart. "I think I'm falling in love with you, Jared."

Jared brings my hand up to his mouth for a kiss. "I'm in love with you, Sophie. I have been since the moment you got into my cab and refused to leave."

I choke back a laugh. "I thought we agreed it was my cab."

Jared chuckles and reaches for the wine bottle. "Let's agree to disagree."

"You're just trying to get me to shut up."

Jared's eyes glitter when he looks at me. "I would never."

I look at him with a big smile on my face.

Chapter Eight: Jared

"You have to put the mask properly," I instruct, patiently. "Look how I'm doing it."

Sophie huffs, her hair plastered to her forehead. "This is too hard."

"Here, why don't I give you a hand?" I reach her, and she pauses before taking off the snorkel mask and tube.

With a smile, I show her how to put it on, and she listens intently the entire time. When I'm done, she releases a deep breath and tries again.

She ducks her head underneath the water, and I wait for a few seconds. Emerging, she is sputtering and gasping for air.

She growls, rips the mask off her face and holds it away from her body. "I don't think snorkeling is for me."

I chuckle and lower myself further into the water. "Why don't you climb on my back, and we can go for a swim?"

Sophie giggles and takes both snorkeling gears. After a brief hesitation, she wraps her legs around my waist and hoists herself up.

I secure her feet and run my hand down the length of her, mostly, bare back, stopping at the strings of her top.

"You know, there's no one out here at this time of day," I whisper, letting my hands fall down to her hips. I give them a firm squeeze and linger. "You could probably take your top off."

Sophie sighs, and her skin breaks out into shivers. "As tempting as that offer is, I don't want to flash some fisherman or something."

I laugh and unhook her feet from around my waist. I spin around to face her, and she wraps herself around me, so our chests are pressed together.

In her red bikini, showing off her tanned, ivory skin, she is even more alluring. It's all I can not to rip her swimsuit off and bury myself in her.

She is studying me, a strange glimmer in her eyes. "What are you thinking?"

I run my fingers down her back, grazing the skin as I do. "How much I want to take your swimsuit off and get you naked."

Sophie blushes. "I'm being serious."

"So am I."

Sophie lifts her chin up and clears her throat. "You want to know what I'm thinking? This is my second favorite vacation that I've ever been on."

I wrap my arms around her waist and rub my nose against hers. "What's your first?"

"When we were little, we went on vacation with my grandparents. It was completely unplanned. My parents just came to pick us up from school, and my grandma and grandpa and the dog were in the backseat, and we kept driving till we reached this coastal town."

I smile. "That sounds beautiful."

"It was." Sophie's expression turns thoughtful. "We stayed in this rental right on the water, and Melanie and I stayed up all night just to watch the sunrise. And in the morning, we went swimming and collected all these seashells. I remember my grandparents playing with us and walking along the water, they were so in love, but this was before my grandma got sick."

I push her hair away from her face and press a kiss to her lips. "I'm sorry you had to go through that, but I'm glad you have that memory of her."

Sophie shakes her head and gives me a small smile. "Me too. She would've liked you."

"Yeah?"

"Absolutely." Sophie links her fingers over my neck and leans back to look at me. Underneath the bright glow of the early morning sun, her skin glistens, giving her a warm ethereal glow. "What's your favorite vacation?"

I pause. "I don't know that I have a favorite vacation, but I do have a favorite memory."

"Tell me."

"When I was younger, before the cancer took my mom away. She showed up to the first apartment I ever owned. It had this huge balcony which used to get a lot of sunlight. We just sat together, talking and laughing until the sun went down."

Sophie's expression turns sad. "Your mom sounds like she was amazing."

"She was. She was a force to be reckoned with, and she didn't let anyone stop her. When she left my dad, there were a lot of dark times. I wondered if she was going to be able to get through it, but she did. It was just the kind of person she was."

Sophie touches a hand to my face, and a shiver races up my spine. "I'm sure she would've been proud of you."

"I like to think so."

Silence settles between us. Sophie wraps herself around me as we float around the water, fused together. When I bring my head to rest against her chest, I can hear the pounding of her heart, wild and unsteady.

I smile and squeeze my eyes shut, marveling at the sense of peace starting within my stomach.

A short while later, Sophie stirs and pulls away from me. She swims back to the shore, and I watch her back.

When she gets out, she tosses her hair over her shoulders and walks over to the towels, her entire body glistening, and her swimsuit clinging to her like a second skin.

She sits down on the towel, stretches her body out and brushes off the sand.

I can't look away. Sophie has well and truly gotten under my skin, and I don't mind. I don't mind one damn bit because I've never felt this way about anyone.

I like that she isn't afraid to call me out on my bullshit or poke fun at me when I'm being too serious.

I like how I feel when I'm around her, like the whole world is mine for the taking.

With a smile, I swim over to the shore and get out. Sophie's eyes stay on me as I walk over to and drop down on the towel, kicking up sand as I did.

She sticks her tongue out at me and uses the other towel to clean herself off.

I shake my head, sending droplets of water all around me.

Sophie rolls her eyes at me. "Do you have to do that here?"

I nod and stretch my legs out in front of me. "Yes."

"There are plenty of other places," Sophie says, pausing to sweep her arms out on either side of her. "No one is here right now."

"But then I wouldn't get to see your cute angry face," I tell her, with a wink. "I wouldn't miss that for the world."

A flush steals across Sophie's neck and cheeks. "You need to get out more."

I lean forward and cup her chin. "Nah, I think I'm good."

With a start, I realize that all I need is the woman in front of me who has brought me back to life in more ways than she knows.

"What's that look for?"

I make my way over to kiss her. "I was just thinking about how lucky I am."

Sophie's eyes are glowing when I draw back to look at her. "Why is that?"

I lower my hand and lace my fingers through hers. "Because I'm here with you."

Silence stretches between us. "I'm lucky too," Sophie whispers.

I study each individual eyelash up close and count the freckles on her face. Wordlessly, Sophie reaches for her bag and rummages through it.

She pulls out a tube of sunscreen and holds it out to me. With a smile, I motion for her to turn around.

After a brief pause, she gives me her back, and I rest the tube between my fingers.

I squeeze a generous amount onto my palms and run my fingers down the length of her back. My fingers dart back up and undo the strings of her top.

Sophie's breath hitches in her throat, but she says nothing.

My heart is hammering against my chest as I spread the gel over every inch of exposed skin, pausing at certain parts to marvel at the smooth and toned skin.

Sophie begins to make low whimpering noises and tilts her head to the side. She twists her arm over her head, and I lean forward, allowing her to grab a fistful of my hair.

"What happened to not wanting to put on a show for everyone?"

Sophie exhales. "No one's here."

I continue to run my fingers down her back. "You won't be able to take it back."

"I know." Sophie breathes, her entire body melting against mine. I press my face to the back of her neck and pepper it with hot, open-mouthed kisses.

Her entire body breaks out into goosebumps, and she shivers. I drape my legs on either side of her and dig my nails into her flesh.

Sophie rubs her back against me, and I make a low growling sound. "You really do know how to drive me crazy."

She giggles and pushes her hair forward. "Good."

I wrap my arms around her stomach and squeeze. "What do you say we take this back to the beach house?"

Abruptly, Sophie stands up and wheels around to face me. She links her fingers over my neck and kisses me.

As I taste sunscreen and sand, my fingers drift down to her waist. She hoists herself up and links her legs over my abdomen.

I smile into the kiss and somehow maneuver us up the steps and into the backyard. She twists a hand behind her back, and without breaking the kiss, pushes the door open.

I set her down on one of the lounge chairs and pause to kick off my flip-flops. Sophie sits up and lets her swim top fall to the floor with a flutter.

My blood is roaring in my ears, and I can't see anything but her. I kneel down in front of her and throw her legs over my shoulders. She wriggles out of her bikini bottom and inches closer to the edge of the chair.

With a smirk, I begin to press hot, open-mouthed kisses along the inside of her thighs, then I move to her center, feeling and tasting every part of her with my tongue, Sophie throws her head back and moans.

I look up, and a strange feeling in the center of my chest unfurls. It grows and expands when Sophie lowers her head and looks directly at me, sending another jolt straight to my core.

She links her fingers over the back of my neck and hoists me up. I pour every inch of emotion that I can into the kiss.

Sophie responds by tightening her legs around my waist. I settle in between her legs, and she rubs herself against me.

One hand darts in between us, and she pushes my swimming shorts down.

With a growl, I position myself at her entrance and brace my hands on either side of her. Sophie falls backward onto the chair and links her legs around my waist.

I position myself at her entrance and bend down to kiss her. In one quick move, I thrust into her.

Sophie tosses her head to the side and cries out my name. I ease out and slam back into her, eliciting another deep and throaty moan. She rakes her fingers over my back, and her breathing quickens.

She makes another whimpering sound, and her hands fall to her sides. I pin her arms over her head and thrust in and out of her.

She is everything, everywhere, all at once. She is all I can see, or taste, or feel. And I can't get enough of her. I want to lose myself in every last part of her.

Each touch, each kiss, each stroke brings me closer and closer to the edge of oblivion. Sophie bucks against me, meeting each thrust with one of her own.

Sweat forms on the back of my neck and pours down my back. I bury my face in the crook of her neck and inhale the salty, sweet smell of her.

She draws me closer and explodes.

Her entire body writhes and spasms as she rides out her high. My own release follows soon after, and Sophie holds me to her as I struggle to catch my breath.

Once I can breathe again, I lower myself onto the chair, and she tucks herself into my side. For a while, we sit there as I listen to the sound of her even breathing.

I never want to let Sophie Davenport go.

Chapter Nine: Sophie

"I know. I'm sorry. I promise I'm not ignoring you." I lower myself onto the couch and stretch my legs out in front of me. "Things have just been hectic with work and everything else."

Melanie laughs. "I know what it's like to have a new man in your life. No need to explain."

I twirl a lock of hair around my finger. "I don't want to jinx it, or anything, but I've got a pretty good feeling about this, Mel."

Melanie gasps. "You've never said that about anyone. It must be serious."

"I think that it is." I throw my head back and stare up at the ceiling. "We've been spending most of our time together, and you know something, I like knowing that I'm going home to him."

"You've moved in together already?"

"No, but we spend most of our time at his place."

"Are you sure this isn't a little fast? You haven't known him for that long."

"I know. I know it hasn't been that long, but it just feels right, Mel. I can't explain it. I just know that I like being with him, and I like who I am when I'm with him."

"Good. That's all that matters. So, are we ever actually going to meet him?"

I sit up straighter, guilt churning in the center of my stomach. "Soon, I hope."

Except I have no idea when.

In the beginning, I wanted to come clean, but now that Jared and I are getting serious, all I want to do is protect our bubble.

We have enough to deal with all of the scrutiny and criticism from his friends and social circle.

The last thing I want is to introduce more stress in the form of our families.

Melanie is never going to understand. And I doubt his children would either.

I hear the security code being punched in, and I swing my legs over the side of the couch. "I've got to go, Mel. Give Cameron my best."

Before she can respond, I hang up and toss the phone onto the coffee table. I place a hand on my hips and smile. "You're late."

Jared kicks the door shut with the back of his leg and sets down his bag.

He tugs his tie; his eyes are moving steadily over my body, staring at the tips of my toes and ending with the edge of the white shirt I'm wearing, leaving very little to the imagination.

"I should be late more often," Jared teases. He throws his tie onto the floor and kicks off his shoes. "I like this look."

"Yeah?"

"Oh, absolutely. You should dress like that all the time," Jared replies, his eyes never leaving my face. He hangs up his jacket and rolls up his sleeves. "You look incredibly sexy."

"I can't wear this outside."

Jared covers the distance between us and places both hands around my waist. "Yeah, you're right. No one's going to get anything done if you look like that. It's safer for the whole world if this look is for my eyes only."

I tilt my head back to look up at him. "How selfless of you."

Jared buries his face in the crook of my neck, the smell of sandalwood and sage washing over me. "Definitely."

I link my fingers over his neck and sigh. "I could get used to this."

He leans back to look at me, and his eyes are glimmering with a strange emotion. "I was hoping you'd say that because I've got something for you."

He removes one hand from around my waist and pats his back pocket.

He pulls out a chain with a key on it. "This is why I'm late. I stopped by to make a copy on the way home."

I glance between the key and his face. "Is that a key to your condo?"

Jared nods. "I want you to move in with me."

I squirm, and he releases his grip on my waist. "I…I don't know what to say. Isn't it a little too soon?"

"I don't feel like it is. Do you?"

I run a hand over my face. "No, but I'm not exactly objective here."

Jared sits on the couch and pats the spot next to him. "What are you worried about?"

I lower myself onto the couch, leaving a few inches of space between us. "You know how I feel about you, Jared, but we've never even talked about the future."

Jared twists to face me, and his brows form a crease. "What is there to talk about? We like being together. Isn't that all that matters?"

I snort and turn, so I'm facing him directly. "You and I both know that's not all that matters. There are other factors too."

Jared arches an eyebrow. "We don't have to talk about them now."

I lean back against the couch and tuck my legs underneath me. "Don't you think that we should? You are asking me to move in with you."

Jared runs a hand over his face and blows out a breath. "I feel like you're making a big deal out of this."

"It is a big deal. You're asking me to give up my apartment."

Jared frowns. "I wasn't aware that you saw it that way. For the record, I'm not asking you to give up anything. You can keep your apartment."

"That's not what this is about."

Jared links his fingers together and folds them in his lap. "Why don't you tell me what this is about then? Because I feel like we are not on the same page."

I rake my fingers through my hair. "I want to be with you, Jared. Just to be clear, it's not about that. I just think we should talk about where this is going before I make a decision like this."

Before I go all in with a man who has the ability to break me.

I already know what'll happen if things don't work out with Jared.

For the first time in my life, I can see an entire future mapped out for us. I can see it so clearly that it fills me with equal amounts of fear and excitement.

I've never felt this way about anyone. And I want Jared to feel the same. I need him to if we have any hope of surviving.

Because I can't be the only one who's willing to go all in with a man who has one foot out the door.

Not again.

Jared unlinks his fingers and moves closer to me. He takes both of my feet and sets them down in his lap.

He leans forward and kisses me, so thoroughly and soundly that when he draws back, I struggle to take air back into my lungs and remember where I am.

He has that kind of effect on me.

"I love you, Sophie. Doesn't that count for something?"

I swallow and utter, "Of course it does. I love you too."

Jared lifts his gaze up, and our eyes meet. "Move in with me."

"I need to know that you're as committed to this relationship as I am," I whisper, trying to ignore the unsteady hammering of my heart. "You know what it's like to be burned, Jared. To have a relationship completely fall apart at the seams, and I know you understand why it's important for us to talk about it."

Jared nods. "I do."

I search his face. "Be honest. Can you see a future with me?"

Jared tilts his head to the side and studies me. "You mean beyond moving in together? Yeah, I can see a future. Hell, I can see myself marrying you, Sophie, if that's what you're asking."

My heart does an odd little somersault. "You have no idea how relieved I am to hear you say that."

Jared's mouth curves into a smile, his face lit up by the soft florescent lighting. "I absolutely want to have a future with you, Sophie. Are you kidding? I thought I was obvious about that."

I release a deep, shaky breath. "Okay."

"I can see us living here together, maybe getting a dog or a cat or something, and in time, I'm sure the kids will get used to you. It'll take some time..."

"What about our own kids?"

Jared's expression shifts, and he draws back. "Soph, I want to have a future with you, but I don't plan on having any more kids."

My heart sputters and dives. "What?"

Jared sets my feet back onto the couch and stands up. "I thought you knew that already. We've talked about this before."

I stumble to my feet, my stomach twisting into knots. "Yeah, but I thought you meant in general that you couldn't see yourself having any more kids."

"You thought I meant until I met the right woman?"

I clasp my hands behind my back and nod. "Well....yeah."

Jared takes a step back and exhales. "I'm sorry, Sophie. But I meant what I said. I've already done the whole kids thing. I'm not looking to do it again. I'm not that young to do that again."

I open and close my mouth, the blood roaring in my ears. "But you…you haven't done it with me."

Jared looks over at me, and his expression softens. "We can get married, Sophie. Isn't that enough?"

Silence settles between us. I move away from him and step into the kitchen.

I push myself up to the tips of my toes and rummage through the cupboard.

In a daze, I fill up a glass of water and down it all before filling it up again.

When I spin back around, Jared is leaning on the other side of the marble counter, watching me intently if not expectantly.

I curl both hands around the glass and set it down. "I don't think it can be enough."

Jared doesn't look away. "You just need some time to process it, that's all. I know it's a big decision to make, so why don't you sleep on it, and we can talk some more in the morning?"

"Don't patronize me, Jared. I'm not a child who needs to be told what to say and what to do."

Jared pushes himself off the counter and folds his arms over his chest. "I'm not trying to treat you like a child. I'm trying to be considerate and understanding."

I grip the counter. "By forcing me to make a decision based on what you want?"

Jared throws his hands up in the air. "I'm not forcing you to do anything, Sophie. I'm just letting you know how I feel."

I shake my head. "So, you're basically giving me an ultimatum."

Jared's expression turns angry. "Don't put words in my mouth. I didn't say that either."

"You might as well have because we both know what's going to happen if I tell you that I want kids. You're either going to only be a part of my life and ignore them, or you walk away. How is that not an ultimatum?"

"It doesn't have to be like this," Jared insists, with a shake of his head. "It's not either or."

"Isn't it? I want kids, Jared. I want kids of my own. I know you've done it all already and don't want any, but I haven't. If I agree with what you want, then I will have this void in my heart for the rest of my life and I might end up blaming you for it. If I can't have any children that's a different story, but if I am able to carry a child and I do want children, then I will be miserable that I can't have my own. I want us to be a complete family. We have love, but why can't we share that with our own kids? Jared, I'm thinking long term not just right now, that we have such an incredible, heartfelt love, and connection. I'm not saying what we have would go away. I'm saying, why not share that with our own kids or, one child at least? We don't have to have more than one."

Jared shoves his hands into his pockets. "I don't know what you want me to say to that."

I push myself off the counter and fold my arms over my chest. "I don't want you to say anything, Jared. I'm just telling you how I feel."

"So am I."

I swallow. "So, what do we do now?"

Jared is standing across the kitchen counter from me staring at the wall in front of him and every few seconds he shifts his gaze and locks eyes with me.

My heart aches seeing the look in his eyes, but I have to know what kind of future he's planning for us.

I don't see him or feel him wanting to give this a try. It seems as if he has made up his mind about starting a family with me.

Chapter Ten: Jared

My fingers move steadily over the keyboard, but I can't see anything. I've been sitting at my desk for hours with a headache in the back of my skull, but it still doesn't make any sense to me.

I've gone over hundreds of emails in the past few hours, all of them standard, and all containing details I know like the back of my hand.

But none of them matters to me. All that matters right now is the woman sitting on the couch a few feet away, with her legs tucked underneath her and a book in her lap.

She'd spent the entire night tossing and turning, and I had felt her gaze on me the entire time. But I hadn't been able to look back at her.

Because I had no idea what to say. I still have no idea what to say.

For the first time since meeting her, Sophie and I aren't on the same page. We might as well be on opposite sides of a mountain.

She has never felt further away from me, even though I know that I can get up, push my chair back, and draw her to me.

Except I know it's not what she wants. Sophie wants something I can't give her, and I can feel the disappointment and fear radiating off her body.

I just can't see myself going through the whole process of having a child.

Don't get me wrong it's an amazing experience, but I just don't want to repeat it again.

I'm not in my 20s or 30s, I'm 48, I got married young and had two kids by age 24, I just can't repeat that at this age.

She's spent the entire morning tiptoeing around me and burying herself in her books and shows. I, on the other hand, have been throwing myself into work in an attempt to fill the void.

It does nothing to dull the pain...or the ache in the center of my chest. With a frown, I push myself away from the desk and stand up.

I stretch my arms up over my head and roll my shoulders. I let them fall to my sides and exhale.

When I bend down to touch my toes, I feel Sophie's eyes on me, quiet and assessing. I glance at her, and she hastily looks away.

She turns a page in her book, and I stand up straighter. "I'm going to go for a run," I announce, a little too loudly. "Do you need anything from outside?"

Sophie responds without looking up. "No, thank you."

I duck into the bedroom and pull on a pair of shorts and a t-shirt.

Once I come back out, Sophie is standing at the double doors of the terrace, a mug of tea in her hands and a wistful expression on her face. She doesn't say anything as I walk past her and head toward the door.

In the doorway, I pause to look back at her and study her, illuminated in the soft glow of the early morning light.

My stomach twists when she tilts her head to the side and looks at me. Our eyes meet and hold. She looks away first and lifts her chin up.

I yank on the knob, step outside, and take the elevator to the first floor. As soon as I'm outside, I plug in my headphones and set off at a brusque pace.

I spend the entire run with the sun on my back and thoughts of Sophie not far from my thoughts.

I keep replaying our conversation over and over in my head until I am covered in sweat, and my lungs are bursting with effort.

Abruptly, I skid to a halt in the middle of the park a few blocks away and place both hands on my thighs. People rush past me in either direction, and I earn a few curious looks.

On the way back, I slow to a trot and try to ignore the twinge in my chest. I'm still no closer to figuring out what to do when I climb up the stairs and nod in the direction of the doorman.

When I punch in the key code and step in, I glance around. I see a note propped up on the kitchen counter, and my heart drops.

Over the next few hours, I alternate between sitting at my desk and staring at my phone.

An untouched box of noodles sits next to me, growing colder and colder by the second.

By the end of the night, it feels as if I'm going to lose it.

When I read Sophie's note to let me know she'll be spending the night at her apartment, I lace up my sneakers and go for another run.

I don't return home until my muscles are aching in protest, and every inch of me is drenched in sweat.

In the shower, I place my hands on either side of the wall and breathe deeply.

But I can smell her everywhere. I carry my pillow and cover into the spare room and throw myself onto the bed.

In spite of my best attempts at falling asleep, I spend the night tossing and turning and staring up at the ceiling.

In the morning, when sleep finally comes, I hear Sophie in the kitchen, her voice dropping to a whisper.

When I come out, she hands me a cup of coffee and steps out onto the terrace without meeting my gaze.

When she comes back in, I sit down at my desk and stare at my screen.

For the rest of the day, we hardly exchange more than a few sentences.

At night, she crawls into bed next to me but curls up into a ball, leaving as much space between us as possible.

In the morning, when my eyes open, and I see that she is curled up against me, I hold her to me and squeeze my eyes shut.

By the fourth day, we still haven't reached a solution.

I can feel Sophie withdrawing from me and retreating into herself, and I have no idea how to stop her…or put our relationship back on track. Not without losing ourselves in the process.

Over the next few days, we fall into a routine where we barely speak and fight over the smallest of things.

Sophie continues to pull away from me, and I throw myself into my work.

By the end of the second week, when I come home, Sophie is leaning against the couch, a suitcase next to her.

I set my bag down by the door, toss my keys onto the table and remove my tie.

"So, that's it?"

Sophie pushes herself off the couch and clears her throat. "I don't see a way out of this, Jared. I'm sorry."

I kick off my shoes and approach her. "Don't leave, Soph. We can find a way to make this work."

Sophie bursts into tears. "I don't think we can. Don't you think that I've tried? I've been wracking my brain trying to think of a solution, but I can't come up with anything."

I cup her face in my hands and press my forehead to hers. "There has to be a solution. There has to be something we haven't thought of. We just need some time."

Sophie sucks in a harsh breath. "We can't keep doing this to each other. Time isn't going to fix this."

I draw back to look at her, and my chest tightens. "What are you saying?"

Sophie takes a step back and hiccoughs. "I'm saying that I've tried. Over the past two weeks, I've done nothing but think about how to make it work, and it's either you have to compromise, or I do."

Silence settles between us. I take an involuntary step back. "So, you just decided that it's over? You weren't even going to talk to me about it?"

Sophie scrubs a hand over her face and sniffs. "Jared, I know what you're trying to do. I know you want to be angry with me—"

"Want to be angry with you? I *am* angry. Because you seem to be forgetting that there are two people in this relationship."

Sophie lifts her chin up and looks directly at me. "Two people who want very different things out of the relationship, or have you forgotten?"

I run a hand through my hair. "No, I refuse to believe that this is how it ends."

"You know that one of the things I love most about you is your fighting spirit," Sophie whispers, her voice trailing off towards the end. "I know you don't like to give up, especially when it comes to people, but there is no way around this."

"No."

Sophie's eyes fill with tears again. "Please, stop. You're making this so much worse than it has to be."

"You're the one who's leaving," I point out, pausing to run a hand over my face.

Dismay and panic wash over me in equal measure, growing stronger and stronger the longer we stand there.

I have no idea what's happening, but I do know that if Sophie walks out that door, it's over for good.

I'm not ready to give up on her. Not without a fight.

"I'm leaving because if I stay, we're going to be unhappy," Sophie tells me, her voice hitching towards the end. "Either you're going to be stuck with kids you didn't want, or I'm going to be stuck in a relationship that doesn't fulfill my needs. I don't want that for either of us."

The blood roars louder in my ears.

Sophie takes a step towards me and another. "We both deserve better, Jared. And we owe it to ourselves to at least try."

I cover the distance between us and take her into my arms. "You can't leave. You can't leave, Soph. I love you."

Sophie buries her face in the crook of my neck. "I love you too."

I squeeze my eyes shut and exhale. "We can figure this out."

A short while later, Sophie squirms and steps out of my arms. She shakes her head and reaches for her bag. "We can't. Sometimes love isn't enough, and sometimes we have to break our own heart. I'm sorry."

With that, she wheels the bag behind her and brushes past me. In the doorway, she pauses to set her keys down on the table and looks back at me. "I hope you find what you're looking for. Take care of yourself, Jared."

I press my mouth into a thin, white line and give her a blank look. As soon as the door shuts, I reach for the nearest object and hurl it at the wall.

The vase smashes into a million pieces, sending shards of glass everywhere.

I scowl and pick up something else, throwing it onto the floor beneath my feet with all my might.

Anger, helplessness and fear all rise within me, all fueling the voices in my head as I see nothing but red.

I yell and scream as I yank and smash things until the living room floor is covered in shards of glass and liquid. When I step onto a piece, a sharp jab of pain races through my body, and I curse.

I run over to the terrace and fling the doors open. Far below, I can barely make out anything, save for vague shapes and colors rushing past in either direction.

I shove both hands into my hair and lower my head.

My body shakes and shudders. I hurry back into the apartment and step over the glass.

I snatch my phone off the counter and dial Sophie's number. It goes straight to voicemail.

I try a few more times, but each time, I get the same result. With a frown, I pour myself a generous amount of whiskey and collapse onto the couch.

For the rest of the night, I alternate between dialing Sophie and staring at the empty fireplace, picturing her face the entire time.

When the sun comes up, I'm sitting there, surrounded by destruction and debris, with no clue what to do next.

Chapter Eleven: Sophie

"You didn't have to fly all the way out here," I mumble between sips of soup. "I can take care of myself."

Melanie frowns and perches on the edge of the bed. "I know, but you're going through one of the worst breakups of your life, and you have the flu."

I sniff. "I appreciate you being here, Mel."

Melanie offers me a small smile. "I know. Also, it's a good excuse for Cameron and I to go on vacation. He's visiting some friends in the city, and I get to see you."

I set down my half-full bowl of chicken noodle soup and sigh. "You haven't told Mom and Dad, have you?"

Melanie pushes her hair out of her face. "No, but you know Mom. It's only a matter of time before she figures it out. Mother's intuition and all."

I throw myself back against the pillow and stare at the ceiling. The same ceiling I've been studying over the past five days.

As if anything is going to change. It looks exactly the same as it always did, with its peeling paint and a lightning shaped crack down the center. With a sigh, I twist onto my side and face the cream-colored wall.

Melanie stands up, mutters something, and picks up the bowl of soup. When she leaves the room, I sit up and watch her back, another lump rising in the back of my throat.

I need to get up. I need to leave the house and get some fresh air.

Yet, each time I think about going outside and facing the prospect of a world without Jared, it hits me all over again. How did I survive without him?

Jared Fox has turned my whole world inside out, and now I have no idea how to put it back.

All I know is that thinking about him hurts. It hurts to breathe, it hurts to eat, and it hurts to go to sleep in an empty bed every night, where the smell of him lingers.

Half of me wants to bottle the scent up and hide it away. The other half of me wants to rip away all of my sheets and everything he's ever touched and burn it all.

I want to scrub my skin raw until I forget what it's like to be touched by him. To be adored by him. To be loved by him.

But I can't do any of that. All I can do is sit in bed, watching the colors of the world outside my window change and pray for the heaviness in my chest to loosen.

Melanie comes back into the room, in her jeans and shirt, carrying a tray of food. "I know you said you're not hungry, but you need to try and eat."

I prop myself up on the pillow and exhale. "I appreciate the effort, Mel, but I just don't feel like it."

"You can't waste away in bed, Soph," Melanie tells me, pausing to set the tray down on the nightstand. "I know you're heartbroken, and everything feels heavy right now, but it will get better."

I swallow and look up at her. "How do you know?"

"Younger sisters know these things." Melanie sits back down on the edge of the bed and tucks her legs underneath her. "The best way to get over the pain is to keep yourself busy. Why don't we go try out that spa you were telling me about?"

I clear my throat. "I can't."

"How about the gym?"

I shrug.

Melanie sighs and leans forward. "Come on, Soph. There's got to be something you want to do."

I suck in a harsh breath. "I need to pack up his things in a box."

Melanie's eyebrows draw together. "Are you sure that's going to make you feel better? Isn't it a little soon to be doing this?"

I shake my head. "It isn't."

Melanie runs a hand over her face. "Are you sure the two of you aren't going to work this out? It's only been a few days. Whatever it is, there has to be a solution."

"We don't have a future together, Mel," I whisper, my eyes darting around the room and looking everywhere else. "I want a family, and he doesn't. And I can't make him want what I want. He'll resent me for it."

And I'd rather have him hate me now than down the line when we have kids. It is for the best. I just need my heart to understand that.

Melanie reaches for my hand and squeezes. "Soph, I'm so sorry."

I look up at her and tears burn the back of my eyes. "You tried to warn me. You tried to tell me that I was moving too fast, but I wouldn't listen."

I wanted to believe that Jared and I were different. I wanted us to be the one in a million beating the odds. I'm an idiot. How could I have been so blind?

It isn't as if Jared has kept it a secret from me. On the contrary, he's been fairly clear about what he wanted from the beginning.

I'm the one who ignored the hidden subtext and charged forward, convincing myself that he would change his mind. That I could make him change his mind. Stupid, stupid girl.

"You need a shower," Melanie announces, after a brief pause.

In spite of my protests, she hoists me up to my feet and pushes me into the bathroom. There she helps me out of my clothes, pushes me into the shower and switches on the water.

Once it heats up, she draws the curtain shut, and I see her vague outline come to a stop in the doorway. "You're going to thank me for this letter."

Hot water cascades down my back and swirls underneath my feet. I lather up soap, my tears mixing with the water. As soon as I push the curtain back, steam follows me out.

Wordlessly, Melanie hands me a towel and looks away. I use both hands to secure it around my waist before pushing my hair out of my eyes.

In a daze, I stumble over to the sink and grip it.

But I can't stand to look at myself in the mirror to see my emptiness and misery looking back at me. Using the back of my hand, I wipe the steam away and glance down.

Slowly, I take several deep breaths to calm my uneven breaths. A wave of nausea washes over me, and my knees buckle.

Melanie helps me to the toilet. Tears are pouring down my face, and my throat burns.

Melanie hands me a tissue, and I wipe my mouth with it and I squeeze my eyes shut when I feel nauseous.

I bring my back to rest against the cool seat cover and release an uneven, shaky breath. "I don't know where this flu came from, but I can't wait for it to leave."

Melanie brushes my hair out of my face and clears her throat. "I don't think it's going away anytime soon."

I pry one eye open and cough. "What do you mean?"

Melanie sighs. "When was the last time you got your period?"

I pause and scrub a hand over my face. "I don't know. Last month, I guess?"

"Are you sure?"

I pause, and panic claws its way through me. "Wait, can you hand me my phone? It's on the other nightstand."

Melanie nods and rises to her feet. She returns a short while later, and I take the phone out of her outstretched hand.

While I do the math, my heart is thumping, and another wave of nausea rises. Suddenly, the phone falls onto the tile beneath my feet, and I bury my face in my hands.

Melanie draws me up to my feet and takes me into the bedroom. After helping me change into a pair of sweatpants and a clean shirt, she sets my phone down next to me.

"There's no need to panic. Not yet at least," Melanie tells me, her dark eyes moving steadily over my face. "I'm going to run and pick up some pregnancy tests just to be on the safe side, okay?"

I nod mutely. While Melanie is gone, I stare at the wall opposite my bed and wonder what I'm supposed to do.

This isn't supposed to be how it unfolds. I shouldn't be having a baby by myself. Jared should be here.

As soon as the thought crosses my mind, I reach for my phone and stop at his name. I stare at it for the longest time and wonder what to do.

The front door clicks open, and I hear Melanie's footsteps. Reluctantly, I set the phone down and throw the covers off.

Melanie is startled to meet me in the doorway to my room. After a quick hug, I carry the plastic bag into my bathroom.

I empty the contents into the sink, heart pounding wildly against my ears. The door creaks open, and I see Melanie through the slit in the door. "I'm here if you need anything."

I swallow and give her a thumbs-up. In silence, I rip open one of the boxes. I skim the instructions and take a deep breath.

My hands are trembling by the time I'm done peeing all three sticks.

Melanie comes into the bathroom and draws me into a hug. She holds me tightly while I count out the minutes.

Two lines emerge on each of the tests. Melanie takes me back into my room as a tremor races through me. She drapes a blanket over my legs and reaches for her phone.

I can't make out anything she's saying. She helps me into a pair of jeans and a T-shirt.

A short while later, she loops her arm through mine, and we walk down the stairs. I'm vaguely aware of the sun on my back and conversation rising and falling around me.

Melanie hails a cab and ushers me into the back seat. She rattles off an address and holds my hand the entire time. Once we reach the cluster of metal buildings on the other side of the city, she pushes me out of the cab.

The smell of disinfectant hits me first, followed closely by the sound of machines beeping. As soon we walk in, Melanie gives them a wave. We are ushered into a small room with a large window overlooking a park.

There is a wooden desk, two chairs, and an exam table that looks pristine. Melanie takes my hand and helps me climb on. A chair makes a screeching sound as she drags it over the floor.

A blonde-haired, blue-eyed doctor comes in, wearing a white lab coat; she flashes me a gentle smile.

I barely feel anything when she draws blood. Melanie takes me back out into the waiting room, and the two of them exchange a few words.

Half an hour later, the doctor gestures and Melanie stands up. When she comes over to me, and I catch a glimpse of her face, I burst into tears. Melanie draws me into another hug and pats my back.

"It's going to be okay, Soph."

"I want this baby," I whisper, into her ear. "I just didn't think it was going to happen like this."

Melanie draws back to look at me. "Are you sure? Are you going to call the father?"

I reach for Melanie's hands and squeeze. "I'm sure and, no, I'm not going to call him. He's made it pretty clear that he doesn't want kids."

And I'm not going to give him a chance to ruin this for me. I want to be a mom, and I'm going to do it, with or without Jared.

Chapter Twelve: Sophie

Four plus years later

"Kayden, put that down."

Kayden folds his arms over his chest and shakes his head. "No."

I sigh, set down the brush and turn to face him.

He is perched on the edge of the stool in front of my dresser, fingers inches away from a bottle of perfume. "Sweetheart, how many times have I told you that you can't play with glass?"

Kayden sticks his bottom lip out. "Mommy, you play with it all the time."

"Because Mommy is an adult who knows how to hold glass," I reply, with a small smile. I step away from the full-length vanity mirror on the other side of the room and toward my son.

His hazel eyes watch me intently until I'm a few feet away. He darts away, hurling himself over the bed as he does.

"You'll never catch me," Kayden says breathlessly.

My lips stretch into a grin. "I'm coming to get you."

With that, I roll onto the mattress and skid to a halt on the other side. When I jump to my feet, Kayden gasps and is frozen to the spot.

I scoop him up into my arms and bury my face against his stomach. He squirms and holds his legs out, but I hold him away from my face.

I throw him over my shoulders and march out of my room.

"I wonder what to do with you."

"Put me down, Mommy," Kayden whispers, in between giggles. "I'll be a good boy."

"No, I'm going to give you to the fairies," I decide after a brief pause. "They'll take you to neverland where you can live with Peter Pan, and the rest of the lost boys."

Kayden throws his head back and laughs. "No, Mommy, no."

I set Kayden down on his feet and ruffle his hair. "Because you'd miss Mommy too much?"

Kayden juts his chin out and gives me a dubious look. "You can come and visit me anytime, Mommy. I want to grow up, so I can go on the big rides at the park."

I choke back a laugh. "So, mommy isn't as important as the rides?"

Kayden's brows furrow. "You're as important, Mommy."

I crouch in front of Kayden, and my eyes move over his face, from his almond shaped eyes to the dark hair that curls at the top of his neck.

Kayden doesn't know it, but he has some of his dad's features, with a few of my mannerisms thrown in.

When I first had him, I couldn't look at him without thinking of Jared. And how much I missed him.

In the beginning, all I could see was the man who had gotten away and taken my heart with him.

Now, over four years later, I don't think of Jared as often. Thankfully, whenever I do, I have Kayden to remind me of why walking away was the right decision.

In spite of the endless sleepless nights, the wailing, and the diaper changes, I feel like I've made it out on the other side.

Kayden makes my life so much better. He is the light of my life, and the reason I get out of bed on days when I can barely keep my eyes open.

I love every minute of being a mom.

"Mommy, do you have to go out?"

I draw Kayden into a hug and rub his back. "We talked about this, honey, remember? Mommy is going to go out with Auntie Mel and Uncle Cameron."

Kayden's expression turns confused. "Can't they come over here?"

"Maybe we will later," I reply, with a smile. "In the meantime, you need to listen to everything Marisa tells you to do, okay? You be a good boy for Mommy."

Kayden sighs and nods. "Okay. Can I have some ice cream?"

"Half a scoop," I tell him, before rising to my feet. "And no trying to trick Marisa into giving you more."

The doorbell rings, and Kayden races to the living room. He hurls himself onto the couch and peeks out from behind the pillows.

My lips twitch as I walk to the door and twist the knob. Marisa, a petite woman with auburn hair and brown eyes stands in the doorway, a backpack slung over her shoulders.

She glances up from her phone and gives me a bright smile.

"Hi, Ms. D."

"Good evening, Marisa," I greet, pausing to push the door open. "How are you?"

"I'm fine, thank you, Ms. D." Marisa steps in and lets the backpack fall to the floor. She pushes it to the side, and her eyes dart over the room. "Where's my little buddy?"

I tilt my head in the direction of the couch. "I have no idea, Marisa. I think he's off helping the tooth fairy again."

Marisa taps her chin. "Wasn't he helping Santa last week?"

I nod. "He's a helpful little boy. You know how much Kayden likes to help other people."

Marisa's lips curve into a smile. "That's right. He does. Oh, well. I guess I'll have to watch the new Lego movie all by myself."

Kayden jumps out from behind the couch, clapping his hands together. "You got the new Lego movie? Mommy, can I watch it? Please."

"When it's done, you need to brush your teeth and let Marisa tuck you in."

Kayden nods, eagerly. "I promise."

"Give Mommy a hug."

Kayden throws himself around my stomach, smelling like soap and baby shampoo. I pat the top of his head and squeeze my eyes shut.

Once the doorbell rings again, Kayden pulls himself away and allows Marisa to lead him away. A strange tightness starts building in my chest as I reach for my purse.

Melanie and Cameron linger in the doorway, bright smiles on their faces. They wave at Kayden, already bouncing up and down on the couch.

I give Marisa a thumbs-up before I step out, and the door clicks shut behind me.

On the way down the stairs, I am filled with the urge to run back upstairs, change out of my clothes, and curl up next to Kayden.

I know I can't do that forever. Since having Kayden, my whole life has been an effort to balance work and being a single mom.

Thankfully, with Melanie and Cameron moving to the city, things have gone a lot smoother. On the days when I feel I'm about to tear my own hair out, Melanie swoops in and saves the day.

I'm incredibly grateful for her, especially because she doesn't ask questions anymore.

After the first year and seeing what a nervous wreck I was, Melanie no longer pushes me to talk about Kayden's dad.

Nor does she question if keeping his existence, a secret is a good idea. She has grown as attached to Kayden as I am, and I know she'll do whatever she can to protect him.

Yet, there are times when I wonder if she suspects, particularly whenever Cameron looks at Kayden too long.

With a slight shake of my head, I step outside and hold the door open for them. The three of us giggle and pile into a cab, with Melanie talking a million miles a minute.

Once it pulls up on the other side of the city to a bar with a pulsing neon sign and a line out front, I already want to go home.

None of this feels like my life anymore. It hasn't in a long time.

Sensing my hesitation, Melanie takes my hand and drags me out of the cab. "Don't even think about making up an excuse to race back home and into your pajamas."

"Comfortable home-wear," I protest, stumbling out behind her. "You said yourself it looks nice."

"Yeah, but it can't be your go to outfit when you're not at work," Melanie protests. Cameron walks up to the bouncer, a tall and bald-headed man with broad shoulders.

He looks over at us and unties the loop. Melanie grins and tugs me along behind her. As soon as we step through the doors, the smell of alcohol and sweat hits me.

Music plays from somewhere while pulsing neon lights flash in and out of focus. I squint and press myself closer to Melanie, who weaves in and out of people with expertise.

We spill out on the other side of the dance floor, near a group of empty booths in the back. Cameron's eyes sweep over the people in attendance before he gestures to a uniformed waiter in the back.

Melanie pulls me down next to her and drapes an arm over my shoulders. "You wanted to come out tonight, remember?"

"I know, but I miss Kayden."

"You are a great mom. You're not any less of a mom for needing a night out," Melanie reminds me, pausing to adjust the straps of her dress. "Besides, your whole life can't be about Kayden or work."

"It's not."

"Netflix shows don't count either," Melanie replies, without looking at me. Once Cameron sits down next to her, she whispers something into his ear. "When was the last time you had a night out?"

"We went out last month, remember?"

Melanie twists to face me and raises an eyebrow. "Are we counting a trip to Costco as an outing? No, Soph. Come on. I mean a real outing where you get dressed up in something that doesn't have holes or looks like it's going to fall apart."

"I wear nice clothes to work," I reply, before offering the waiter a polite smile. I lift the drink up to my lips and sniff. "You know I was watching this true crime documentary the other day about roofies in drinks..."

Melissa groans and smacks her forehead. "Soph, you're my sister, and I love you, but no. We didn't drag you out here so we can talk about whatever your latest obsession is."

I take a small sip of my drink and make a face. "You're right. I should check on Kayden."

"It's been fifteen minutes." Melanie plucks the phone out of my hands. "He's fine. Marisa will call if anything goes wrong. You've left him with her before."

"Yeah, whenever I've had work events."

Melanie sets my phone down on the table and makes a sweeping hand gesture. "Think of this as a work event if it'll make you feel better."

I sit up straighter and glance around the club, taking in the row of booths in the back and the tightly packed dance floor, where people are gyrating against each other.

I glance back at my sister and Cameron who are cuddled against each other and whispering.

A lump rise in my throat when Cameron reaches out and tucks a lock of hair behind Melanie's ear. She giggles and laces her fingers through his.

I down the rest of my drink and signal for another. Slowly, I let my fingers glide over the table and close over the phone.

"Don't even think about it," Melanie warns without looking at me. "Fun, remember? We're celebrating you getting one of the biggest clients of your career."

I groan and set the phone back in my pocket. "Fine."

Melanie and Cameron hold their drinks up and touch their glasses to mine. "Here's to Sophie, the best single mom and successful career woman in the world."

I didn't belong in this world anymore, not with a three plus-year-old at home. And I didn't mind one bit.

Most nights, I like curling up on the couch with my laptop and a glass of wine while Kayden watches TV.

At the end of every night, I look forward to scooping him up into my arms and tucking him in.

And every time, without fail, Kayden asks for a bedtime story and rests his head against my chest while I read.

I miss him so much it's making my chest hurt and fills my stomach with knots.

Until Kayden came along, I had no idea it was possible to feel this strongly about someone. I almost feel bad for Jared for missing out on his son's life.

For the rest of the night, I remain in my seat, drinking through a straw and sneaking a glance at my sister and her cool husband.

When I finally make it back home, Kayden is fast asleep. I change into my pajamas, sneak into bed next to him, and switch off my alarm for the weekend.

Chapter Thirteen: Jared

"Mr. Chang, I can assure you that you are our top priority." I turn in my chair and stare through my window, relishing the view of the city's towering skyline.

On the other line, Mr. Chang continues to speak, airing out his grievances like there's no tomorrow. With a frown, I spin my chair back around and stare through the glass doors at my assistant.

Mitchel sinks lower in his seat and avoids my gaze. Heads will roll when I get off the phone, and he knows it. As soon as Mr. Chang hangs up, I buzz Mitchel in.

Through the glass, I see him reluctantly stand up and rap on the door. When I motion for him to come in, he pauses and straightens his tie.

He plasters a smile on his face and pushes the door.

"You wanted to see me, Mr. Fox?"

"Yes, I want to know who's the idiot who spooked Mr. Chang."

"I don't know who was in charge of the project while you were on business, sir," Mitchel replies, without meeting my gaze. "Would you like me to find out?"

My frown deepens. "Yes, I need to do some serious damage control. Can you set up a business dinner with him at *Chez Francoise*?"

Mitchel nods and types something into the tablet. "Yes, sir."

"Let them know the reservation is for me, so they can book us a table for today."

Mitchel swallows. "Yes, sir."

"And for God's sake, find out who was in charge of the project and bring them in. Now."

Mitchel nods and scurries out of the office. On his way out, he pulls the door shut behind him, plunging me into silence, save for the whirring of the AC in the background.

I stand up, roll my shoulders and pour myself some water.

Over the rim, I eye the office space behind Mitchel, filled with rows and rows of cubicles, all with well-dressed employees hard at work behind their desks.

It isn't their fault I'm in a bad mood. Having spent most of the night schmoozing up to potential clients had taken its toll, and I'd wanted to reward myself.

With a shake of my head, I set my glass down and open the first drawer. I place two painkillers in my mouth to ward off the pounding headache at the back of my skull.

I'm on my second glass of water when Mitchel knocks on the door and gestures to Braden, a transfer from another tech company.

His blonde hair glistens, and he strides into my office in his expensive custom suit and sits across from me.

I don't take my eyes off of him as I lean over the desk.

"I want to know what dumbass school you went to that taught you that it's fine to spook a potential investor."

Braden's smug look fell as he sat up straighter. "Mr. Fox—"

I hold up a hand. "I'm not done talking. When I'm done, you'll know. I've just spent my entire morning on the phone, trying to convince Mr. Chang that we are still worth investing in. He's one of the richest men in East Asia, and you nearly cost us that investment."

Braden squirms and swallows. Slowly, I sit back down and link my fingers together. "I don't care what you did to skate by during business school or tech school or whatever damn school you went to, in my company, this is not how we do things. Is that understood?"

Braden clears his throat. "Yes, sir."

"Get out." I gesture to the door and lean back in my chair. "Figure out a way to make this better."

I sigh and close my eyes as my head is pounding in my ears.

·♥·♥·♥·♥·♥·

"Thank you, Giles." I push my door open and step out onto the curb. Once the door clicks shut behind me, I slide my phone into my pocket.

The double doors are pushed open once they see me, and I'm greeted with smiles and nods. The dark-haired uniformed maître d straightens when he sees me and leads me past rows and rows of tables.

He steps in front of a closed curtain and pushes it aside.

The music is quieter there. Only a few tables are available, most of which are unoccupied.

Mr. Chang is already at his table, perusing the menu while a blonde-haired waitress in a black and white uniform pours wine.

I slip the maître d some money and whisper something into her ear.

With a smile, I approach Mr. Chang, taking one hand out of my pocket. "Please order whatever you want, Mr. Chang. It's my treat."

"I took the liberty of ordering the most expensive wine on the menu," Mr. Chang replies, without looking up. "I hope you don't mind."

My chair is pulled out with a screech, and I sit down. "Not at all."

Mr. Chang glances up, his dark brown eyes assessing me openly. "Good. It's the least you can do to make it up to me."

I nod and reach for my glass of wine. "Whatever you need."

Out of the corner of my eye, I see a flash of movement, followed by quick laughter. I turn to the sound and see two women a few tables away whispering to each other.

One of them looks up, and I see her profile, a long, slender neck and wisps of dark hair. When she looks up at the waiter and smiles, my heart stops in my chest.

All of a sudden, a rush of emotions pours into my heart and my being and, I am taken away for a moment, forgetting where I am and all I can see was her.

Sophie looks even more beautiful than I remember. She is nodding along to what the waiter is saying, and he's gawking at her.

My stomach does an odd little lurch when she stands up and adjusts the straps of her dress. She gives me her back and strides in the direction of the bathroom.

I lean sideways in my side, hoping to catch another glimpse of her before she disappears. I see her long legs, clad in dark heels before the door swings shut.

I swallow and sit up straighter. "I can make a suggestion if you don't know what you want to order."

Mr. Chang glances at me, lips twitching in amusement. "A man as decisive as yourself shouldn't let a woman like that get away."

I nearly choke on my drink. "I beg your pardon?"

Mr. Chang sets his menu down and adjusts his glasses. "I saw you gawk at the young lady who went into the bathroom. You know her, right?"

I clear my throat. "I used to know her."

"No reason you can't continue your acquaintance," Mr. Chang responds, with a smile. "Second chances don't come around often. From where I'm standing and from the look on your face when you saw her and from your reaction and body language, I can tell, she still has your heart."

I take a long sip of my wine and feel it burn a path down my throat. "I doubt she wants to talk to me. We didn't leave on the best of terms."

And I've spent the past four plus years trying to forget her. Seeing her again, after all this time, is like having a jolt go through me.

Like I've been dragged back down to the reality of my life without her; it's been an endless slew of business meetings and trips.

I've been trying to forget I ever knew Sophie all to dull the ache in my chest, and the pain of having her walk away from me.

Having our paths cross during a business dinner no less, feels surreal. As if I'm watching it happen to someone else.

Yet, I can't deny that the pull is still here, drawing me to her.

Mr. Chang picks up his own drink and eyes me over the rim. "This could be the chance you've been waiting for, don't you think?"

Sophie comes back out of the bathroom, her silver eyes downcast and a smile hovering on the edge of her lips. She tucks a lock of hair behind her ear and glances up.

When she looks over at me and our eyes meet, she comes to a complete stop in the middle of the room. I push my chair back, set my napkin down on the table, and walk over to her.

Her hand clutching the phone falls to her side. "What are you doing here?"

"Hello to you too."

Sophie blinks and stands up straighter. "Hi."

I stop a few feet away and offer the wait staff an apologetic smile. "Hi. You look great."

Sophie tilts her head to the side. "Thank you."

"Sorry to interrupt your dinner." I nod in the direction of her companion, a short woman in a sparkling dress with streaks of silver in her hair. "I saw you from across the room, and I had to come over."

Sophie's brows furrow. "Oh."

"It's really good to see you," I continue, with an easy smile. "You look really good, Soph."

"Thanks. So do you."

"I'm on a business dinner." I tilt my head in the direction of Mr. Chang, who is watching us intently. "Big client. He's a big fan of the place."

"It's got great food."

"It does."

"It's hard to get a table," Sophie adds, pausing to shift from one foot to the other. "My client knows the chef, so that's how we got in."

"Client?"

"I'm her lawyer," Sophie clarifies, with a smile in the woman's direction. "Speaking of, I should probably get to our dinner."

I take a step toward her. "We should get together sometime and catch up. I can't believe I'm running into you again."

Sophie pauses. "I don't know."

I take two steps toward her and look into her eyes. "For old time's sake. Please. It'll be my treat."

Her floral perfume wafts over to me, and it takes me back in time. I resist the urge to take her into my arms and kiss her.

She has as much of an effect on me as she did all those years ago.

Goddamn it. Why are you still in my system, Sophie Davenport? Why haven't I forgotten about you?

Sophie sighs and takes a step back. "Okay."

"Still have the same number?"

Sophie nods, a strange look on her face. "Yeah."

"I'll call you to set up the details." I lean forward and press my lips to her cheek. "I can't wait to see you again."

Her breath hitches in her throat. When I pull away, I see a glimmer of something familiar. She holds herself still as I walk away, my eyes never leaving her face.

When I sit back down, I'm in a much better mood and can't stop finding excuses to glance over at Sophie who is blushing as she takes her seat.

All through the night, I can't stop thinking about her or ignoring the swarm of butterflies erupting in my stomach in her presence.

When I return to an empty apartment after a long and fruitful dinner, Sophie is still on my mind, and I know why.

Seeing her today has made me realize that I've never stopped loving her. She's the one who got away, and now that we've crossed paths again, I am not letting her go.

Come hell or high water.

Chapter Fourteen: Sophie

"How do these look?" I hold up the earrings and look over at Melanie, who is hovering in the doorway, arms folded over her chest. "Too gaudy, right?"

Melanie sighs. "It depends on what you're going for."

I set the earrings down on the dresser and rummage through my box for another pair. "I'm not going for anything. He wouldn't let me get back to dinner, so I said yes to shut him up."

I'd allowed myself to forget how it felt to be around Jared. A part of me doesn't want to forget again.

Melanie steps into the room and glances over her shoulders. "Are you sure it's a good idea to be going out with him again? This is Kayden's father, right?"

I nod and reach for another pair of earrings. "Yeah, it is."

"I want you to be happy, Soph. I do. I just don't know if getting involved again with the man who broke your heart is a good idea."

"We wanted different things back then, Mel."

Melanie glances into the mirror and holds my gaze. "And how about right now? You don't even know if the two of you are on the same page."

"It's what dinner is for." I twist to face her and give her an unconvincing smile. "Trust me, I know what I'm doing."

Except I don't, and Melanie is right. I don't have a single clue what I'm supposed to do…or how I'm supposed to behave.

All I know is that I've spent the past few hours rifling through my clothes and groaning while Cameron and Melanie play with Kayden.

Laughter rises and falls around me, punctuated by the occasional shriek from Kayden. I glance over at Melanie who shrugs and pokes her head out the door.

"They're fine," Melanie assures me, after a brief pause. "They're playing some kind of wrestling game."

"If my son gets injured while rough housing with Cameron—"

"I know, I know. Way ahead of you, sis." Melanie spins back around to face me and gives me a once over. "You look good. Just remember to take things slow and don't let him get under your skin again."

I give her a thumbs up. "Don't worry."

Melanie exhales. "For the record, I still think it's a terrible idea."

"Duly noted."

Together we step out of my room and into the blue colored hallway. Cameron is on the carpeted floor of the living room, with Kayden on top of him, his arms held out on either side of him.

As soon as he sees me, my son leaps off of Cameron and rushes over to me. He throws himself against my stomach, and I make a startled grunting sound in response.

"You're getting so much stronger, sweetheart." I ruffle his hair and lower my head to look at him. "You'll be good for Aunty Mel and Uncle Cam?"

Kayden draws back to look at me. "I will. Mommy, why do you look so nice?"

"Your mom always looks nice," Melanie interrupts. "She's going out for some grown-up bonding time."

I shoot Melanie a dirty look. "Aunt Mel is kidding."

"Come on, bud," Cameron calls, from his spot on the floor. "There's some more moves that I want to show you."

Kayden glances between the two of us and gives me a dubious look. He hurries back to where Cameron is, and the two of them fall backward onto the floor.

Kayden knocks the breath out of Cameron who wheezes and coughs. Melanie shakes her head and rifles through the fridge.

"Can you bring us back dessert?"

I snatch my purse off of the table next to the front door. "Yeah, if I can. Got any preferences?"

Melanie's head emerges, and her expression turns thoughtful. "I can't decide between chocolate cake or cheesecake. Maybe both."

I shove my feet into a pair of ballet flats. "Message me when you decide. Call if you need anything."

Melanie blows me a kiss and waves my comment away.

I race down the stairs, taking them two at a time. Once I'm outside, a blast of warm air hits me in the face. I glance down both sides of the street and gesture to a cab, crawling through a thin mist.

As soon as I settle in, I lean back and send Jared a quick message. People and trees rush past in either direction, a blur of colors and shapes.

When the cab pulls up on the other side of the city outside a cluster of fancy looking restaurants, with a line of people outside, the butterflies in my stomach return.

With a sigh, I stumble out of the cab and glance up. At the top of the stairs, I am greeted by a uniformed doorman who straightens when I give Jared's name.

He holds the door open for me, and I duck inside, the soft strings of jazz music hitting me first.

My eyes adjust to the dim lightning, and I see rows of booths lined up on either side of the restaurant. A huge glass display behind the bar is full of bottles.

Conversation rises and falls around me. Uniformed waiters and waitresses rush past in either direction. I try not to gawk as I am shown to a secluded spot in the back, overlooking the kitchen doors.

Someone pulls my chair out, and I sit down. When I reach for the menu, Jared comes in, looking handsome in a pair of dark jeans and a button-down shirt.

His hair is windswept, and his smile sends a shiver racing up my spine.

"Thanks for asking me here," I tell him, as soon as he sits down. "I've been wanting to go, but it's almost impossible to get a reservation."

Jared picks up the menu and scans it. "It is. I know the owner though, so he owes me a favor."

"You know everyone, don't you?"

Jared blinks and sits up straighter. "It's part of the job. How's being a lawyer?"

I shrug. "Same old."

Jared sets his menu down and looks directly at me. "You're a lot more beautiful than I remember, Soph. And that's saying a lot."

I blush and hide behind my menu. "Thank you. You're not looking so bad yourself."

Jared flashes me another smile. "Thanks."

I clear my throat. "So, what's good here?"

"Other than you? You should try the risotto."

"Still as charming as ever," I mutter, mostly to myself. "You haven't changed a bit."

Jared gestures to a waiter and orders a bottle of wine. "You've changed a lot. All good things though."

I set down the menu. "I'm surprised you asked me to dinner. The last time we saw each other—"

Jared holds a hand up and leans back in his chair. "Let's not talk about that. All that matters is that we're here."

A blonde waiter appears and pours us both a generous amount of wine. Jared picks up his glass and touches it to mine.

We spend the whole night catching up and making small talk. The food is delicious, and a steady supply of wine leaves me giddy and light-headed.

When dinner is over, Jared ushers me outside into a black car parked by the curb.

He reaches for my hand when we lean back against the seats. "I've missed you."

I blow out a breath. "You shouldn't say stuff like that."

Jared turns to face me, his hazel eyes molten. "Why not?"

"Because I'm going to do something stupid."

"I'm not stopping you." His fingers glid up my arm and stop at my collarbone. "What do you want to do, Sophie?"

I make a low strangled noise and something in me snaps when Jared's hand moves further, and he begins to stroke my neck.

I throw one leg over him, then the other, so I'm straddling him. Jared leans forward and presses a button that lifts the partition.

As soon as it clicks into place, he cups the back of my neck and kisses me.

He kisses me so thoroughly and passionately that it leaves my head spinning. I place one hand on either side of him and buck, molten hot desire pooling within me.

Jared growls into my mouth as his hands move to the hem of my dress. In seconds, it has been hiked up enough to reveal his target. Goosebumps break out across my flesh.

I am falling, hurtling over the edge, but I don't even care.

All I care about is how good it feels to be touched by Jared. To have his fingers move over my skin, worshipping every inch like he's committing it to memory.

I grind against him, prompting him to emit another low noise that reverberates inside of my head.

I keep one hand pressed against the chair while the other reaches to fumble with his belt buckle. It loosens with a whoosh sound, and I grab his zipper.

"I can see that you've missed me too," Jared says, into my skin. He presses hot, open-mouthed kisses against my neck and over my jaw, and pauses to tug on my earlobes. "Fuck, you taste even better than I remember."

His zipper slides down, and I lift myself up. "Less talking."

Jared leans back to look at me, and his eyes don't leave my face as he rips my underwear apart with one hand.

He wiggles, and I position myself on top of him. When I sink into him, something bursts within me. I am gasping for breath. Jared sinks his fingers into my bare skin and eases out.

"Oh, God. Oh, *Jared*." I throw my head back and moan.

Jared buries his face in the crook of my neck. "You feel better too. Fuck, Sophie. I can tell how much you've missed me."

I dig my nails into the seat behind us and squeeze my eyes shut. "You feel so good."

Jared draws his lips back and sinks his teeth into my neck. "We're just getting started. I'm going to make you remember how good it felt between us."

I begin to bounce up and down, my pulse quickening as I do. Jared keeps one hand on my waist, pinning me on top of him while the other moves up to my breasts.

He lowers the straps and flicks each nipple. He takes one between his teeth, sucking and biting until I am about to burst. Once he switches to the other, I throw my head back and whimper.

"That's it, baby," Jared murmurs, his voice like music to my ears. "That's my girl."

I feel myself climbing higher and higher, racing towards oblivion. Each stroke, each touch, each kiss pushing me closer and closer to the edge.

I lace my fingers through his hair, my movements growing faster and more frenzied. Suddenly, it doesn't matter that we broke up some time ago or that all of the reasons why still matter.

All I can think about is how good it feels to be with him again...to feel his body pressed against mine.

Jared exerts more thrusts, and the force of my orgasm rips through me, leaving me gasping and panting. I am writhing and spasming as I cling to him for dear life.

My vision turns white as Jared's own release comes next, and his body shudders with pleasure. He gives a few more thrusts before going still against me.

I place my head against his chest, over the pounding of his heart, and try to remember how to breathe.

Jared cups the back of my neck and laces his fingers through my hair. For a while, we sit there till our breathing turns even, and I roll off of him.

Fuck. What have I done?

Chapter Fifteen: Sophie

"You have nothing to worry about, Ms. Rodriguez. We can get this sort out."

"Are you sure?"

I snap the file shut and glance up at her. "Absolutely. It won't even go to court."

Ms. Rodriguez breathes a sigh of relief and sinks into the chair opposite my desk. "Are you sure?"

"I've been doing this for a long time, Ms. Rodriguez. You're in good hands."

Ms. Rodriguez sets her purse down in her lap and looks up at me. "My son did tell me that you're good. I wanted to see it for myself."

"I'm happy to help," I reply, with a smile. "Let me just go over the paperwork, and I'll get in back in touch with you. How does that sound?"

Ms. Rodriguez nods and reaches into her purse. She pulls out a box of tissues and wipes her face. "You have no idea how thankful I am."

"No problem at all, Ms. Rodriguez. Would you like something before you leave?"

Ms. Rodriguez stands up and adjusts the strap of her purse. "No, thank you, Ms. Davenport. You'll be in touch, right?"

"I will." I offer her another smile and reach for the ringing phone on my desk. "Thank you for coming in, Mrs. Rodriguez."

"Pretty sure my name isn't Mrs. Rodriguez."

I give Ms. Rodriguez a small smile as she pulls the door shut behind her. "I'm pretty sure that isn't your name either. Unless you have something you want to tell me."

Jared laughs. "You mean other than the fact that I had a great time last night? When can I see you again?"

I switch the phone to my other ear and spin around in my chair. "I don't know. I've got a lot of work to do."

"What about during your lunch break?"

I draw my bottom lip between my teeth and chew. "Jared, I..."

"No overthinking," Jared interrupts. "We both admitted that we missed each other. That's all we need to know."

Except he and I both know that isn't true.

The reason we can't be together still exists.

"Look, I called because I wanted to hear your voice but also, I wanted to see if you were free for lunch."

I stare at the pile of paperwork on my desk and frown. "I don't think I'm going to be able to leave the office for lunch today. I've got a lot of paperwork."

"Good thing I thought ahead." Jared's voice drifts and comes back on. "I remember the kind of sandwich you like."

"What do you mean?"

Jared's face appears in my doorway, making my stomach do somersaults. I drop the phone and jump to my feet.

He pushes the door open and steps in, devastatingly handsome in his suit and tie, with two plastic bags in his hand.

With a smile, he sets them down on the floor and leans over the desk to kiss me.

In a daze, I sit back down on one of the empty chairs and face him. "What are you doing here?"

"I got us lunch." Jared begins to take food out of the bags. "I got you two tuna on rye, a diet soda and fries."

My stomach grumbles in response. "You didn't have to."

"I know how hard you work," Jared replies, without looking at me. "And yes, I got an extra pack of fries in case you're still hungry."

I lace my fingers together and place my hands in my lap. "I can't believe you remember all of that."

Jared gives me a meaningful look over his shoulders. "I remember a lot more than that."

A blush creeps up my neck and stains my cheeks. "It's been years. I'm sure you've forgotten a few things."

Jared turns to face me and sits down opposite me. He hands me my sandwiches without looking away. "You're probably right."

I bite into my sandwich. "You got these from the regular place down the street?"

Jared nods and unwraps his own turkey sub. "And they are just as good as I remember."

I chew and swallow a piece. "You haven't been recently?"

Jared shakes his head and cracks open a can of soda. "Not since you and I broke up."

"I'm sorry you felt you had to avoid it."

Jared unwraps more of his sandwich and rips off a big piece. "I'm not. It's closer to your office. Wouldn't have been fair of me to monopolize it."

I swallow. "Thanks."

"You're welcome."

Jared glances around, taking in the large window overlooking the city, the door with my name on it, and the AC whirring steadily in the background. "You've got a much nicer office."

I nod. "Yeah, I've had a lot of good clients since then. Do you remember Mr. Rogers?"

Jared smiles and nods. "I remember how often he used to call you during weekends."

I chuckle. "Yeah, I forgot how annoying that was, but yeah. He followed through. Gave me a bonus and introduced me to a whole bunch of his friends."

Jared takes a sip of his drink. "I'm really glad everything worked out, Soph. I wanted to reach out and see how you were..."

I take another bite of my sandwich, and it tastes great. "It's probably better that you didn't."

Jared frowns. "Is it?"

I open my mouth to respond, and my phone interrupts. When I glance over at my desk and see Kayden's picture flash across my screen, I drop my sandwich.

Hastily, I snatch the phone off the desk and reject the call before Jared can catch a glimpse.

It's one thing for the two of us to reconnect, and it's another for me to tell him about Kayden, especially when I have no idea if he wants to be a part of his son's life.

A part of me still feels guilty for keeping it from Jared, without even giving him a chance to prove me wrong. He deserves to be a part of Kayden's life.

"I think it's not such a bad thing that you and I are reconnecting," Jared continues, in a quieter voice. "It wasn't all bad."

I blink and shove my phone into my pocket. "It wasn't bad at all."

Jared gives me a smile. "Are you just saying that because I got you lunch?"

I take another bite of my sandwich and clear my throat. "Obviously."

Jared chuckles and reaches for a fry. "Good. Thanks for being honest."

I look away and set the sandwich down. "I should probably get back to work. I've got a lot of paperwork to go through."

"You've barely finished your sandwich," Jared protests. "Don't you at least want some of your fries?"

I stand up and brush the crumbs off my skirt. "I can reheat them later."

Jared wraps his sandwich, and I can feel his eyes on me. "Is this because of what I said about us reconnecting?"

I sigh and step behind my desk. "In part. Look, I think we shouldn't rush into things, but I really do have work to finish."

Jared sets his sandwich down and leans over the desk. "Fair enough. We'll take it as slow as you want. How about dinner later in the week?"

I pause and glance over at him. "Ummm..."

Jared flashes me another smile, sending a shiver up my spine. "Come on, one dinner. I won't bite unless you want me to."

I choke back a laugh. "Okay, alright. One dinner."

Jared stands up and his eyes sweep over me, starting with the top of my head and ending at the bottom of my toes.

Once he lifts his gaze back up to mine, a molten feeling emerges in the center of my stomach, along with a familiar ache in the center of my chest, an ache that had been with me ever since the two of us broke up.

I've spent the past few years trying to shove it all down. I can't believe Jared is able to bring all of it to the surface with one look. Shit.

As soon as Jared leaves, I sink into my chair and bury my face in my hands. Jared's cologne lingers in the air: the distinct smell of sandalwood and old spice.

I squeeze my eyes shut, inhale and try to remember all of the reasons why jumping back into something isn't a good idea.

All I can think about is how good we were. All of the laughs and stolen kisses we shared…and the way he made me feel.

Having spent the past few years convincing myself that I didn't need Jared and was perfectly capable of moving on without him, I am beginning to realize how dishonest I was with myself. How dishonest I still am.

I don't need Jared in my life, but I can't deny that I want him so badly that it hurts to breathe.

With a sigh, I turn my attention back to the screen. Over the next few hours, I respond to emails and answer phone calls.

By the time I make it home, the sun is dipping below the horizon, and I have a dull pounding in the back of my head.

In the doorway to my apartment, I pause and run a hand through my hair. As a matter of fact, I plaster a smile on my face.

Inside, the lights are dimmed, and the TV is turned down low. The babysitter's face appears, bathed in a soft white glow. She jumps to her feet and gestures to Kayden's room: the door is left slightly ajar.

I smile, reach into my wallet and motion to her. When she leaves, I slip off my shoes and leave them by the door.

On the tips of my toes, I creep over to Kayden's room and stand in the doorway.

He is sound asleep, the covers already pushed down to his waist, his arms flung on either side of him. With a smile, I step into the room and hold my breath.

I kneel on the carpet, push his hair out of his eyes, and press a kiss to his forehead. He stirs and flips onto his side.

When I make my way back to my own room, my phone is blinking, and Jared's name flashes across the screen. I don't answer.

I spend the whole night tossing and turning and wondering what to do.

For the rest of the week, Jared comes up with excuses to stop by, usually with lunch and flowers.

By the end of the week, when it's time for us to go out to dinner, I can't think of an excuse not to go…until we arrive at the restaurant, and it's teeming with his colleagues, all of them wearing sour faces and casting suspicious glances in our direction.

"I'm sorry," Jared says, once we're seated. "I didn't realize they were going to be here."

I set my napkin down on my lap. "It's fine."

"You know how particular they are about food," Jared continues, with a quick glance around the room. "And this is one of the best restaurants in the city."

I reach for my glass of wine and eye him over the rim. "I'm sure they could find more places to eat if they lowered their standards."

Jared snorts. "Yeah, that's not going to happen. You know how they are. Once they find something they like, it's hard for them to let go."

"And if they don't like something, good luck convincing them they're wrong," I mutter, pausing to take a long sip of my drink. "Yeah, I remember."

I remember a little too well what it's like to try and win their approval, like jumping through hoops made of fire only to realize they were the ones to light them.

Jared's world is exactly the same as it's always been. But I'm not the same person I was, and I have no idea where that leaves us.

Jared reaches across the table and takes my hand in his. "You look beautiful tonight."

My lips lift into a half smile. "Thank you. You don't look so bad yourself."

I am getting better at picking and choosing my battles and filtering out the white noise, but it doesn't change the fact that being here is bringing it all back.

All of the reasons why being with Jared isn't easy, like walking a fine tripwire at all times.

It's reminding me of why I walked away from him to begin with.

Chapter Sixteen: Jared

"I'll call you when I'm ready to go. Thank you, William." I push the car door open and pause in the middle of the sidewalk.

I reach into the car and pull the containers towards me. When I straighten my back, I pat my pocket, smiling at the box tucked in neatly.

I straighten my back and kick the door shut.

I can't wait to see the look on Sophie's face when she sees her gift.

After spending the past few days trying to pick out the perfect bracelet, I'm sure this is the one for her. With a smile, I tilt my head back and glance up at the building.

I see a glimpse of Sophie's outline through the window curtains. She has her phone pressed to her ear and is waving.

When she moves away, I give a slight shake of my head and stare straight ahead.

I push my way through the double doors and nod at the security team. Once I'm in the elevator, I shift from one foot to the other and tap my foot impatiently.

Finally, the doors open and I step out, the smell from the containers wafting up my nostrils. I earn a few smiles and curious looks, but I ignore them, making a beeline for Sophie's office.

Through the glass, I see her pacing the length of her office, a vision in her knee length black skirt and white button-down blouse.

She spins around, her phone still pressed to her ear; she sees me. I give her a bright smile, and her expression changes as a brief flicker of panic crossing her features.

She shoves the phone into her pocket and pulls the door open. "Hey."

"I got us the usual," I tell her, pausing to press my lips to her cheek. "You smell nice."

Sophie blushes and glances over my shoulders. "Thanks. I completely forgot you were coming today."

"That's okay."

Sophie lets the door fall shut behind me. "I have an idea. Why don't we take the food and go eat somewhere? There's a park nearby."

I set down the containers and turn to face her. "I thought you wanted to stay nearby in case they need you."

Sophie links her fingers. "I should. I mean, I do, but I think they can survive for an hour or something."

I frown. "Is everything okay? You look a little pale?"

Sophie glances over her shoulders and back at me. "Yeah, I just don't want to get in trouble with my boss, you know."

I nod. "Yeah, of course. We can go right now if you want."

Sophie breathes a sigh of relief. "Great. Let me just make a quick phone call. It'll only take a—"

The door to her office bursts open, and a little boy with unruly dark hair races in, a plastic bag clutched to his chest. "Mommy, look at all the treats Marge got me from the vending machine."

What the fuck? Did he just call her Mommy? I feel like the rug has been ripped out from under me while I remain rooted to the spot.

Sophie whips around and crouches in front of him. "You can't have all of that right now, sweetheart. You know it'll spoil your appetite."

The little boy pouts and blinks up at her. "Can't I have some of them?"

Sophie sighs. "Just one. Mommy has something important she has to do. Is it okay if you spend some more time with Aunty Marge?"

The little boy nods and glances over at me. He looks back at his mom, a furrow appearing between his hazel, almond shaped eyes. "Who's that, Mommy?"

My heart is pounding loudly against my ears. Sophie has a lot of explaining to do.

Sophie rises to her feet. "An old friend. Come on, let's go find Marge."

Without looking at me, she leaves the office.

Through the glass, I see her place both hands on her son's shoulders and steer him in the direction of a large desk, where a woman with glasses and streaks of silver hair is sitting.

After a brief conversation, Sophie ruffles her son's hair and presses a kiss to it. She hurries back to her office, heels clicking steadily against the floor.

As soon as she emerges in the doorway, she shoots me an apologetic look.

In silence, she lowers the blinds and shuts the door. "I know what this looks like, but this is not how I wanted you to find out."

I jolt to attention and fold my arms over my chest. "Really? Because it sounds like you have a son you didn't bother to tell me about."

Sophie straightens her back. "We were just getting to know each other. I didn't know if I should."

I stare at her. "Is he mine?"

Sophie pauses and clears her throat to say, "Yes."

My hands fall to my sides, and I take a step back. "Jesus Christ, Sophie. Why didn't you reach out? Don't you think I had the right to know?"

I can't believe how much I've missed out on all already. Almost four fucking years of his life to be exact.

"I wanted to tell you," Sophie replies, with a lift of her chin. "I just wasn't sure how."

I run a hand over my face. "When did you find out?"

Sophie's eyes dart around the room. "A few days after we broke up."

A surge of anger rises through me. "So, you found out right away. You could've told me. We could've figured it out—"

Sophie scoffs, and she snaps to attention. "Why? Because you were inspiring a lot of confidence before? You and I both know what would've happened, Jared."

I frown. "What are you implying?"

I don't like the way she is looking at me or the fact that she knows exactly what she's talking about.

Sophie and I weren't together for long, but she's one of the few people alive who knows who I am.

"I'm not implying anything," Sophie replies, after a lengthy pause. "I'm just telling you the truth."

"The truth? That's rich. You want to talk about the truth? How about the fact that I have a fucking son out there, and you didn't think I had the right to know?"

Sophie throws her arms out to her sides. "What do you want from me, Jared? I did the best that I could."

"That's not fucking good enough."

Sophie's eyes flash as she takes a step toward me. "You seem to be forgetting why we broke up in the first place, or did you forget?"

"I didn't forget—"

Sophie takes another step towards me, her face twisted in fury. "So, how was it going to work, huh? You didn't want to have children, remember? And I did, so what were we going to do?"

"God! I don't fucking know."

Sophie points a finger at me and bristles. "Exactly, but I do. I've known from the moment I got the news. I've wanted Kayden since the moment I learned about him."

I swallow. "That's not fair. I would've been there."

Sophie lowers her finger and shakes her head. "Because you would've felt obligated to be there…not because you actually wanted to be there. I didn't want that kind of life for him."

My blood is pounding louder this time. "So, you took the choice away from me?"

"I didn't have a choice, Jared. You made it clear that you didn't want children, and I did. I made the best decision I could to protect my son."

"Our son," I correct, pausing to run a hand over my face in dismay. "He's my son too."

And although I'm still struggling to come to terms with the fact that I'm a father again, I know that I want to be given a chance.

I want to try, even if the thought terrifies me. Silence stretches between us.

"I know how I felt back then," I add, with a shake of my head. "And I know what I said."

Sophie lifts her gaze up to mine and studies me. "So, what does that mean?"

"I don't know."

Sophie sighs and takes a step back. "I think you should leave. Kayden doesn't need someone in his life who isn't sure."

"Soph—"

She takes a step back and places a hand on the door. "When you've figured it out, give me a call. In the meantime, I think it would be better if we stop seeing each other for a while."

"So, that's it? You're just going to give up?"

Sophie stiffens. "I'm not giving up. I'm putting my son first. I will always put him first."

I stare at her for a few more seconds. I stir to action, shoving both hands into my pockets. My feet feel like lead as I brush past her and into the hallway.

On my way to the elevator, I glance at Marge's desk and see Kayden, his head thrown back mid-laugh and a wrinkle between his brows.

He looks so much like me.

The doors shut, and I'm left to the mercy of my thoughts. Once on the sidewalk, I wander around aimlessly till I find myself at the park.

I select a bench closer to the gate and sit down. For a while, I watch the other families come in, laughing and smiling together. It makes me feel worse about everything.

I hate that Sophie is right. I don't know if knowing about Kayden would've made a difference, not when I'd been adamant about not being a dad again.

Considering I already have two kids with a woman I barely speak to, I'm not looking forward to repeating the experience.

I know that Sophie is different. She's already a better mother than my ex.

Fuck. Why couldn't she have been honest with me? *You were pretty clear about how you felt, Jared. She did make the best decision she could with the information she had. It was never about hurting you.*

When my phone rings, pulling me out of my thoughts, I rise to my feet. In a daze, I walk back to Sophie's office building and get into my car.

The driver takes me back to my office. As I linger outside on the sidewalk, a strange restlessness takes hold of me. Finally, I force myself inside, my head held high.

In my office, I peel off my jacket and drape it over the back of the chair. I spend the rest of the day answering calls and sending emails.

Neither Sophie nor Kayden leave my mind the entire time. All I can think about is all of the things I've missed out on and all of the opportunities we could've been a family.

Would you have even wanted to be a family? Be honest. Are you more upset that Kayden grew up without a father, or that Sophie kept it from you?

With a frown, I sit back down behind my desk and stare at my screen.

When my assistant knocks, I realize the sun is dipping below the horizon, and I've been in the same position for two hours.

I get up, roll my shoulders and power off my laptop. In the elevator, I pull out my phone and stare at Sophie's name.

Once the doors open, I shove my phone back into my pocket and press my lips together. The car ride home is lonely and quiet and full of the ghosts of what could've been.

Chapter Seventeen: Sophie

"Mommy." Kayden launches himself onto my bed and curls up next to me. "You look sad."

I tuck him into my side and ruffle his hair. "I'm not sad, sweetheart. Mommy just has a lot on her mind."

Kayden tilts his head up to look at me. "Is it because of your friend?"

I glance down at him and push his hair out of his face. "Friend? What has Aunty Mel been telling you?"

Kayden's eyebrows drew together. "She said you went to see an old friend, and he means a lot to you."

"He does." I nod and sigh. "Or he did. I don't know if he wants to be my friend anymore." Nor am I entirely sure I can blame him.

I have kept Kayden from him, with good reason, but the facts remain the same.

As far as Jared is concerned, I made my decision based on my own feelings and didn't pause to consider that he might've had a change of heart.

Had I been too hasty? Valued my own feelings over my son's well-being?

Kayden nuzzles against me. "He's silly, Mommy. You're a good Mommy. I want to be your friend."

My heart swells with emotion as I drape an arm over my son and squeeze him hard. He giggles when I begin to tickle him.

A short while later, breathless and with tears of laughter running down our cheeks, we settle back against my bed.

Kayden pauses to change into his pajamas. Once he has them on, I draw the blanket up to our chins and switch on the TV.

It isn't long before Kayden is sound asleep with a cartoon playing in the background. On the nightstand, my phone buzzes and brings me to the present with a jolt.

Slowly, I remove my arm from around Kayden's shoulders and lean forward. When I see Melanie's name flash across the screen, my stomach gives an odd little dip.

With a sigh, I crawl out of the bed and towards the room.

The door creaks open, and I hold my breath. Kayden flips onto his side, but his breathing is even and steady.

In the hallway, I breathe a sigh of relief before I answer the call and press the phone to my ear. "Hey."

"Hey, why are you whispering? Is everything okay?"

"Kayden is asleep," I murmur, pausing to glance over my shoulders, peering through the slit in the door. "He's been extra clingy the past few days."

"He probably senses your bad mood," Melanie replies, pausing to yell something into the background. "So, you ready to tell me what really happened?"

"Well, what can I say?" I wander into the living room and perch on the edge of the couch. "Kayden's dad found out about him, and he's pissed."

Melanie blows out a breath. "I thought you said he didn't want kids, and he wouldn't have wanted to be a part of Kayden's life."

I run a hand over my face. "That's what he told me when we broke up. He was pretty clear, Mel. I made the best decision I could."

Melanie sighs. "Except, he kind of has a point."

I stand up and step into the kitchen. After finding an empty glass, I fill it up with water and take a long sip. "Come on, Mel. Not you too. What was I supposed to do? Beg him to want Kayden? You know it wouldn't have worked out well."

"Maybe it would've, you don't know for sure."

I take another sip of my water and frown. "I wasn't willing to take that chance. Kayden deserves a parent that actually wants him, not someone who would be forcing himself to be there."

"Are you absolutely sure he wouldn't have wanted to be there?"

I set my glass down with a little more force than necessary. "Well, no. No one is absolutely sure of anything, but I do know that I made the best decision I could with the information I had."

"I know you did. Now there's nothing to do but deal with the consequences."

I swallow. "Do you think he'll try to take Kayden away? What if he tries to file for full custody or something? He's rich and well-connected. I don't think I can beat him in court."

"Whoa, slow down. No one said anything about him wanting to take Kayden away. Take a deep breath, okay?"

I release a deep, shaky breath. "Sorry, I'm just freaking out because I don't know what he's planning on doing."

Or how I'm meant to react to any of this. For years, I've wondered what it would be like to tell Jared the truth, and now that he does, a part of me wants to take it back.

I like living in a bubble with Kayden and not worrying about having our hearts broken.

Having Jared back in my life is not only opening us up to that possibility, but it's also unchartered territory for me.

I know what to expect as a single mom, and I have no idea if I even have it in me to co-parent with Jared. Especially not when I still feel drawn to him.

"He'll reach out when he's ready," Melanie says, pausing to yell something else into the background. "Look, from everything you've told me about him, he's a good guy. The two of you just weren't on the same page. Maybe it's time to get on the same page."

I brace myself against the counter. "I don't know what that's going to look like. It's just been Kayden and I for a long time."

"Look at it this way, having Kayden around is probably going to be a good thing. He's been wondering about his dad for a while, and I know you don't want to keep that from him."

I exhale. "I don't."

"Take it one day at a time and wait to see what he says. I'm sure it'll all work out."

·♥·♥·♥·♥·♥·

Jared

"It's open," I call out, pausing to use the back of my hand to wipe the sweat off of my face. "I'm in the gym."

Cameron's face emerges in the doorway, a cautious look on his face. "Am I interrupting anything?"

I pick up a remote and switch off the music. "No, I've just got a lot on my mind."

"Big business deal?"

I shake my head. "No, actually. It's something personal. I reconnected with an ex recently, and I discovered she's been hiding something from me."

I still can't wrap my head around the fact that I have another son. One I've never met. I've only gotten a brief glimpse of his face, so I don't even know what he looks like exactly.

All I know is that I haven't been able to stop thinking about him or Sophie for the past few days.

Every meeting, every phone call, and every email is littered with thoughts of them and what the past few years could've been like.

How did we end up here? Am I really the one to blame for not making Sophie feel safe enough to come clean?

I lament the fact that I didn't handle things differently. Still, I am also furious at Sophie for not even giving me a chance to redeem myself.

Rather than come clean and let the chips fall where they may, she tried to control the outcome and we're in this mess.

Her fear of rejection is the reason we're in this mess. I'm not sure I'm ready to get over that.

Cameron steps into the room and clears his throat. "We got another sibling we don't know about or something?"

I pick up my water bottle and lift it up to my lips. "How would you feel if you did?"

"I think it would be cool. Not sure how Olive would feel about it that way."

"How is your sister?"

Cameron shoves a hand into the pocket of his jeans. "She's okay. You know how busy work keeps her."

I nod and take a long sip of my water. "That's good."

A moment later, Cameron lifts his gaze up to mine and frowns. "How would you feel about having another kid? I didn't even know it was something you wanted."

"It's not or it wasn't, but now I don't know."

I have no idea if I have it in me to do it all over again. While my relationship with Cameron is good, my experience with Olive has taught me not to get too comfortable.

The last thing I need is both of them turning on me because of my relationship with Sophie. Cameron, especially, isn't going to understand.

The lines are pretty clear with him, and I know I've crossed one. But a part of me hopes he can learn to make his peace with it, for Kayden's sake.

Fuck. I've only known about him for a few days, and I'm already protective of my son, wondering what it would be like to have him in my life.

I remember what it was like with Cameron, spending days at football stadiums and sneaking into the yard to eat hot dogs and ice cream. I want to do all of that with Kayden. I have so much to make up for.

My earlier anger returns, and I clutch the bottle in my hand. "Anyway, I don't know if it matters much."

Cameron raises an eyebrow. "Why not?"

"Things are complicated with my ex," I reply, after a brief pause. "There's a lot to figure out."

"Are we still talking about a hypothetical situation?"

I shake my head.

Cameron releases a deep breath. "Oh, well in that case, I guess you'd better figure things out quickly. The longer you wait, the harder it'll be."

Slowly, I set my water down on the treadmill behind me. "You're being really calm about this."

"I'm still trying to process it all," Cameron replies, with a shake of his head. "What are you going to do?"

"I'm not sure," I admit.

I know I want to be in Kayden's life, but I don't know if Sophie will let me.

Hell, I don't even know if I'm going to be able to give him what he needs.

Not only am I no longer the young father I once was, full of energy and exuberance, but Sophie and I haven't even discussed the dynamics of our relationship.

I thought the hardest part about reconnecting would be finding a compromise that wouldn't leave either of us miserable.

Fucking hell. How did we end up here?

Cameron claps me on the back. "Well, whatever is happening, I'm sure you'll figure something out."

"You've got a lot of faith in your old man."

Cameron withdraws his arm and shrugs. "That's because I know you'll do the right thing."

I offer Cameron a smile. "Anyway, I'm sure you didn't come here to hear your old man whine and complain. How's everything with Melanie? You two good?"

Cameron nods, and his expression relaxes. "Yeah, we're good. Ever since we moved closer to her family, things have gotten better. Melanie likes being closer to Sophie."

"That's nice."

Suddenly, I'm jealous that my son and his wife have been in my son's life. They have years' worth of knowledge that I don't.

A voice in my head reminds me that Sophie didn't do this to hurt me. Considering the circumstances of our breakup and how vehement I'd been about not wanting children, I understand why, but it's so hard to accept.

Had the roles been reversed, I'm not sure I wouldn't have done the same thing.

With a slight shake of my head, I lead Cameron out of my home gym and to the kitchen. I rummage through the fridge and pull out two bottles of beer.

I feel Cameron's eyes on me the whole time, but I say nothing. I wonder if Cameron is suspecting anything and that's why he's really here to get some information from me or if he knows who my ex is.

All I can think about is that little boy and whether or not I'm ready to have him in my life.

While Kayden is no longer a baby, I'm not under any delusion regarding the level of commitment and responsibility that goes into taking care of a three or a four year old. Especially one who has no idea who I am.

Will he even want me in his life? I have no idea what Sophie has told him about me, or if she's even mentioned me at all.

All I know is that the longer I sit across from Cameron in my living room, drinking my beer and making small talk, the more conflicted I feel.

This isn't how I imagined running into Sophie again would be like. Not even close.

When we finish our drinks, I get us two more bottles, and we sit out on the balcony, watching the dying of the light and talking about nothing in particular.

A few hours later, when Cameron leaves, I'm no closer to figuring out what to do about Kayden.

But I do know one thing is the thought of losing Sophie again isn't something I'm willing to entertain.

Chapter Eighteen: Sophie

"Are you sure it's okay that he's spending the night here?"

Melanie waves my comment away. "Soph, why are you acting like he hasn't spent the night before? He'll be fine. You know how much he loves spending time with Cameron."

"Still third wheeling it, huh?"

Melanie kicks the refrigerator door shut with the back of her leg. "When he's older, he'll learn to appreciate me more. Right now, he likes Cameron better because they get to wrestle and fart - or whatever other boy humor they like to indulge in."

I wrinkle my nose. "Thanks for that image."

Melanie pats my back on her way past. "That's for calling me a third wheel. Look, you have nothing to worry about. We've got a new movie for him to watch, popcorn, and snacks. The whole works."

"And you're sure you and Cameron don't have anything important?"

Melanie stops in the middle of the living room and glances over at me. "Why do I feel like you're trying to talk yourself out of tonight?"

I shift from one foot to the other. "Because I absolutely am. I don't even know why I agreed to this."

Melanie raises an eyebrow. "I thought you wanted to clear the air with his father?"

"I do, but I'm not sure if that's what we're doing tonight," I reply, after a brief pause. "I mean, it's only been a week since we last talked. What if I don't like what he has to say?"

Melanie places one hand on either side of my shoulders. "Then, at least, you'll know for sure. It's better to know than to wonder, right?"

I search Melanie's face. "What if he doesn't want to be a part of Kayden's life?"

In the background, Kayden shrieks with laughter as Cameron chases him around the living room, pausing to throw the boy over his shoulders.

My gaze switches, and I smile at the sight of Kayden dangling upside down and banging on Cameron's back.

To his credit, Cameron doesn't lose his grip or falter until they reach the couch, and they both fall backward onto it in a heap.

"If he doesn't, it's his loss," Melanie whispers, her expression turning serious. "You and Kayden have made it without him, and you've got us. If he walks away, it'll be his loss."

"What will I tell Kayden?"

Melanie gives my shoulders another squeeze and releases me. "When he's older, you'll figure it out. For now, all you have to do is go back home and wait for Kayden's father to come, okay?"

I take a breath and nod. "Okay, I can do that."

Melanie steers me in the direction of the door and hands me my purse. "Call me if you need me...and have fun."

With that, she slams the door in my face. I linger in the hallway outside their apartment. I straighten my back, go down the stairs, and in a daze, make my way to the car.

I keep fidgeting and checking the mirror. I can't sit still. Once I reach my apartment, I change out of my jeans and shirt into a knee-length dress.

I rake my fingers through my hair and dim the lights, giving the apartment a warm, ethereal glow.

When I'm done, I light a few candles and set them up in strategic spots, allowing the smell of lavender and vanilla to fill up the house.

I perch on the edge of the couch and toss my hair back over my shoulders. Okay, Soph. You can do this. He's just coming over to talk; he wouldn't have suggested passing by the apartment if it wasn't a good thing.

The doorbell rings, and my heart nearly jumps out of my chest. I race to the door and open it with a little more enthusiasm than required.

Jared is standing on the other side, in a pair of dark jeans and a button-down shirt. He is brandishing a bouquet of flowers.

"Hi, these are for you." He holds the flowers out to me and flashes a smile.

"Thank you." I sniff the flowers and step to the side, beckoning him in. Once he brushes past me, I catch a whiff of his cologne, a mixture of sandalwood and sage.

It makes my heart do an odd little flip. I'm leading Jared into the living room, pausing to leave the flowers on the counter.

He sits opposite of me and dutifully folds his hands in his lap. "Thanks for agreeing to meet."

I swallow to alleviate the dryness in my throat. "I wasn't sure you'd call."

"I know I took a while. I'm sorry about that. It's just a lot to take, and I wanted to be sure I didn't rush into anything."

I nod. "I understand."

Jared shifts closer to me. "First of all, I want to apologize for my reaction in the office. It was way out of line, and you deserve better."

I shake my head. "I understand why you were upset. You were right. I should've told you. I did want to. In the beginning, I even picked up the phone a few times, but I...I couldn't risk it, Jared. I'm sorry."

Jared's expression softens. "Sophie, I know I was pissed at you for not telling me, but I've thought about it, and I get why you did it. You were trying to protect Kayden. I would've done the same thing."

My heart sputters and misses a beat. "You think so?"

Jared's lips lift into a half smile. "Yeah, I do. I love my kids, and I would do anything for them. I'm not mad at you anymore."

"Are you sure about that?"

Jared draws closer and takes both of my hands in his. "Do you want me to keep being mad at you? It kind of sounds like you are."

I let out a nervous laugh. "No, it's not that. I just want to be sure that you're actually over it and not just saying that."

Jared chuckles. "Don't worry. I'm not just saying that. I've had some time to think, and I know what I want to do."

My breath hitches in my throat. "What do you want to do?"

"I want to be part of Kayden's life," Jared confesses, his gaze settling on my face. "I know what I said, but I don't feel that way anymore. He's my son too."

I search Jared's face. "If you're not one hundred percent sure—"

"I am," Jared interrupts, giving me a solemn look. "And I want to be a part of your life too. I want us to be a family, Sophie. All three of us."

I exhale. "It's not going to be easy."

"It will be well worth it," Jared whispers, before approaching me. He kisses me so thoroughly that it takes my breath away. I sigh, and my fingers move to the back of his neck.

I lace my fingers through his hair and move closer, my heart pounding in my ears. Jared cups the back of my neck, sending shivers racing up and down my spine.

I taste every last part of his mouth and realize I've been starving for him and his touch, and the way he makes me feel.

Jared makes a low noise in the back of his throat, and his fingers move to my dress. He deftly moves it aside and presses himself against me.

He wrenches his lips away and hoists me up to my feet. In one quick move, he pulls the dress up over my head and throws it over his shoulders, leaving me exposed.

Wordlessly, he unhooks my bra. Slowly, he gets down on his knees. Using his mouth, he pulls my panties down over my thighs and down to my feet. I place both hands on his shoulders and step out of them.

Jared presses hot, open-mouthed kisses along the inside of my thighs and stops when he reaches my center.

My fingers wind around a strand of hair and I inhale sharply. "That feels good."

"We're just getting started," Jared promises, his stubble tickling my sensitive skin. "Hold on tight."

With that, he pushes me, so I fall backward against the couch. Once I sit up, placing my elbows on either side of me, he throws my legs over his shoulders.

Suddenly, his mouth is all over me, his tongue doing strange things to my insides. I throw my head back, tightening the grip on the back of his neck, and I moan.

His tongue darts out and licks a path up then moves sideways, sending wave after wave of pleasure coursing through me.

My lungs are bursting with effort. Each stroke, each touch, each kiss drives me closer and closer to the edge. I am holding onto Jared for dear life, and I don't even care.

The sound of his heavy breathing and mine reverberates inside my head.

I grip the back of his neck tighter, and he redoubles his effort.

I climb higher and higher until the force of an orgasm rips through me, leaving me gasping and writhing against the couch.

The couch dips and creaks until I go completely still, spots dancing in my field of vision.

Jared hoists me up, settles me against the couch, and looms over me. He bends down to kiss me, pouring every ounce of emotion he can muster up into the kiss.

In a daze, I kiss him back, my hands digging into his shoulders. With a growl, he nudges my legs apart and settles in between them, positioning himself at my entrance.

When he thrusts into me, I gasp and wrench my lips away.

I slide my fingers over his back as he eases out and then slams back into me.

Jared buries his face in the crook of my neck, and I inhale the smell of musk and sweat, a heady combination that makes my heart race.

We begin to move together, slowly at first, as if we have all the time in the world. I am learning every crevice and everything that makes him react.

He is worshipping me with his body. I am at his mercy, and I don't care.

I am hurtling toward the edge and tighten my legs around his waist. He throws his head back and continues to thrust with animal abandon.

Suddenly, I am falling again, writhing and spasming as I come undone beneath him. He dips his head and takes my nipple between his teeth.

I am trying to remember how to breathe when he moves to the other nipple and bites down hard.

I cry out his name, and his own release follows, making his body jerk and shudder. He exhales, collapses against me and doesn't move.

I squeeze my eyes shut, hold him to me, and feel the hammering of his heart. Sometime later, he rolls off me and collapses against the couch.

He tucks me into him and presses a kiss to the side of my head. "That was amazing."

I place my head in the crook of his neck and throw a leg over him. "Tell me about it."

Jared drapes an arm over my shoulders and squeezes. "I can't believe how lucky I am."

I stir and look up at him. "I'm glad you feel that way."

Jared looks down at me, and his smile lights up his entire face. "I do, and I can't wait for the three of us to be family. I'm a little out of practice when it comes to being a dad, but I'll do my best."

I kiss the tip of his nose. "That's all anyone can do. Don't worry. Kayden is going to love you."

Jared pulls me into a hug, I close my eyes, lean on him, and inhale his scent. I try to take in everything that has been happening in the last few weeks.

Chapter Nineteen: Jared

"Are you sure I shouldn't get him anything?"

Sophie laughs. "You've asked me that a few times already. My answer hasn't changed from ten minutes ago."

"I'm in front of a toy store," I replied, pausing to switch my phone to the other ear. "I can be in and out in a few minutes."

"Jared, it really is fine. Just get over here, so you can meet him already."

I stand up straighter and study the toy store in front of me, taking up at least half the block.

Large windows show off their impressive display and a steady stream of people are coming in and out.

A part of me wants to ignore Sophie, go in and pick a few things. The other half of me knows that when it comes to Kayden, at least for now, she is the expert.

She knows him far better than I do, but I am looking to remedy that. And I think a toy is a good place to start.

"I can get something small. Like a toy car or something."

"He's got plenty of toys," Sophie informs me, pausing to whisper to someone in the background. "Tell you what, why don't you get him a tub of his favorite ice cream?"

I nod and turn my back on the toy store. "What kind of ice cream does he like?"

"Either mint chocolate chip or bubble gum."

"How about you?"

"I like lemon or vanilla, but you don't have to get me anything."

"I'll be there soon."

With that, I hang up the call and walk to the nearest ice cream shop, joining the queue of people at the register.

When I reach the front, I am nervous, sweat forming on the back of my neck. I take the tub and cones stacked on top in a large bag and leave the store.

A while later, I reach Sophie's apartment building on the other side of the city.

On the way up, I ignore the tight knots in my stomach. Once I reach her front door, I pause, shift from one foot to the other, and knock.

Moments later, I hear the shuffle of feet, followed by giggling, and Sophie's door creaks open, revealing a red-faced Sophie with streaks of flour on her face and in her hair. She looks at the flowers, then my face and smiles.

"Hi."

"Hi, I know you told me not to bring anything, but I couldn't show up empty-handed," I reply, with a smile. "Beautiful flowers"

Sophie blushes and pushes the door open. "We wanted to make a cake, but we couldn't decide on that or cupcakes."

I step inside and wait for her to close the door. I give her a quick peck on the cheeks, and she takes the bag out of my hands. "I think this is a good look on you."

Sophie laughs and sets the flowers down on the counter. "Sure, why not? Kayden, can you pause the movie for a second?"

Kayden stops jumping up and picks the remote up off the table. He points at the TV mounted above the mantel and turns around.

Once he reaches us, and I get a closer look, I am taken aback all over again.

With his hazel, almond-shaped eyes and dark hair curling at the nape of his neck, he looks so much like me at his age, down to the dimple in the middle of his chin.

Kayden stands next to Sophie and tugs on her shirt. "Mommy, who is this?"

"Do you remember how Aunt Mel told you about mommy's special friend?"

Kayden nods. She crouches in front of him and pushes his hair out of his eyes. "This is mommy's special friend. He wanted to meet you. What do you think? Do you want to meet him too?"

Kayden looks over me and holds his hands out. "Hi, I'm Kayden. What's your name?"

My throat closes up when I take his hand. It takes me a few tries to get the words out. "My name's Jared. It's nice to meet you, Kayden. I've been waiting to meet you for a very long time."

Kayden tilts his head to the side. "Really?"

I swallow and release his hand. "Oh, yeah, absolutely. Your mom's told me all about what a great kid you are. I even stopped and got your favorite ice cream."

Kayden's mouth split into a grin. "Mommy, can I have some?"

Sophie rose to her feet and draped an arm over her shoulders. "Why don't you take Jared and show him your toy collection, and I'll get you the ice cream. How does that sound?"

Kayden nods eagerly. "Okay, can I have two scoops instead of one?"

Sophie chuckles and pats his head. "One and a half, and you have to put away your toys after."

Kayden takes my hand and leads me into the living room.

He takes me to the box of toys in the corner and flings his arms out in glee. "These are my toys. Mommy, Aunty Mel and Uncle Cameron buy me toys all the time. What do you think?"

I smile. "I think that's a really nice collection. Can you take some of them out and show me?"

Kayden reaches for one of the boxes and sets it down on the carpet. "Okay, but Mommy says you have to be careful with the toys, so they don't break. And we have to put them away when we're done."

"Of course." I lower myself onto the carpet and tuck my legs underneath me. "You know, I used to have toy boxes just like you."

Kayden pries the lid open and pulls out an action figure. "Did you like superheroes too?"

"I loved Spider-Man. Who's your favorite?"

Kayden's eyes lit up as he rummages through the box and pulls out a Spider-Man action figure. "Me too. I have the bed sheets, and Mommy got me the costume for Halloween last year."

"Can I tell you a secret?"

Kayden moves closer, and his expression turns solemn, "Yes."

I glance over my shoulders and shift closer to him. "It'll be our little secret then."

Kayden presses a finger to his lips.

"When I was younger, I tried to get a spider to bite me, so I could be just like Spider-Man," I whispered. "Do you know what the spider told me?"

Kayden shook his head. "No, what did the spider say?"

"It told me that if I wanted to get super-powers I have to listen to Mommy and be a good boy because mommies are the real superheroes."

Kayden nods, seriously. "Wow! Really! How did he know?"

"Because all mommies are superheroes," I tell him, with a quick look in Sophie's direction. She stood behind the kitchen counter, scooping up ice cream and humming to herself. "Especially your mom."

Kayden smiles. "I know she is. Do you like Mommy?"

I glance back at him and clear my throat. "Yeah, I really do. Your mommy and I have known each other for a long time, and I knew from the moment I met her that she was special."

Kayden hands me his Spider-Man toy and stands up. "I'm going to get my lightsaber to show it to you."

"I can't wait," I say, to his retreating back. He darts off. With a smile, I approach Sophie and stand on the other side of the counter. "Soph, you've done a wonderful job with him. He's a great kid."

"You've only known him for five minutes," Sophie teases, pausing to lick some ice cream off of her wrist. "He is pretty great though, isn't he?"

"Thank you for letting me meet him."

Sophie looks up at me and her expression softens. "Will you help me with the ice cream? I thought we could play a board game or something."

I help her carry the cones, and we go into the living room. "What kind of board games does Kayden like?"

"He likes Connect Four, Battleship and Twister."

I set the tray with snacks and soda down on the coffee table. "I happen to be amazing at Twister."

"Yes!" Kayden returns, his cheeks flush with color, and his glittering with impatience. He swings his lightsaber around. "Mommy isn't very good at Twister, so we don't play that often."

"Hey," Sophie protests, pausing to hand Kayden his cone. "That's not a very nice thing to say. Mommy isn't as flexible as she used to be. Someday when you're older, you'll understand."

Kayden licks his cone and gives Sophie an apologetic look. "I'm sorry, Mommy."

"You have to give me five hugs to make it up to me," Sophie teases, with a twinkle in her eye. "What do you think?"

Kayden eyes her over his cone and nods. "Okay."

Sophie draws him in for a hug and looks up at me. Something warm and unfamiliar unfurls in the center of my chest when I see them together like that.

When we settle down to play Twister, Kayden is buzzing with excitement and barely able to keep still.

Sophie and I have a few mishaps where we nearly knock each other over, and it takes every ounce of self-control not to pull her to me and kiss her.

Since Kayden is with her, I'm trying to respect her boundaries. At least until he's more comfortable with me around.

By the end of the game, it's only Kayden and me. My muscles are aching in protest. Yet, the determined gleam in his eyes and the delight on his face make it all worth it.

And when my muscles quiver and give out, making me crumple into a heap on the floor, Kayden lets out a whoop of delight and dances around the living room.

Sophie holds her hand out and smiles at me. "Not so easy keeping up with a kid, is it?"

I wince and let her pull me to my feet. "I think I might have pulled a muscle."

"I've got ointment for that," Sophie tells me, with a wink. "I'll sneak you some later."

I squeeze her hand. "My hero."

Sophie blushes and withdraws her hand. "How would you feel about a movie tonight?"

Kayden stops jumping around and hurries back to where we're standing. "Can I pick the movie?"

"Sure," Sophie replies. "You have to put away your toys and the board game first, deal?"

"Deal."

Suddenly, Kayden is zipping around the room at an alarmingly high speed, picking up and setting things down with a loud clattering.

When he's done, he lowers himself onto the carpet and tucks his legs underneath him.

He gives Sophie an expectant look, and she steps forward with a smile. "I'm going to get the movie started and make some popcorn."

Kayden claps his hands together. "Extra butter, please."

Sophie ruffles his hair and places a kiss on top of his head. "Alright, sweetheart."

With that, she steps into the kitchen, and I follow. I watch as she opens and closes several cupboards, taking out a pot, a jar of corn and a container of butter.

I smile as she sets it down on the stove and turns the heat down.

Once she spins around to face me, a soft smile hovering on the edge of her lips, my heart gives an odd little flutter. "I'm having a lot of fun."

Sophie grips the counter and snorts. "Sure, you wouldn't prefer one of your fancy parties or dinners?"

"Absolutely not," I reply, with a smile. "There's nowhere else I'd rather be, Soph. A night in with you and Kayden is exactly what I need."

Sophie smiles big and nods. I can see satisfaction written all over her face. I'm happy that she is happy.

Chapter Twenty: Sophie

"Here, why don't we use this color?" Jared stretches his arms over his head and pauses. "Oh, I like your suggestion much better."

Kayden glances up at him and grins. "You'll like it."

He takes the crayon Kayden holds out and cradles it in his hand. "I'll definitely try."

Kayden turns his attention to the sheet laid out underneath him. The two of them are sitting side by side on the carpet, a pile of toys on one side and a box of crayons on the other.

For the past hour, I've been rereading the same paragraph in my book, trying to give them their space.

Except I can't stop looking over at them and marveling at how easy and effortless parenting is for Jared. He's slipped right into the role, and it fits him like a glove.

Over the past ten days, every fear and doubt I've carried around over Jared's involvement in Kayden's life has faded.

Not only has he proven himself to be a kind and attentive father, spending hours playing with Kayden and listening to all of his stories with patience, but he's also gone out of his way to help me as well.

On the days when I come home tired, Jared takes over tidying up and cooking.

I still can't quite believe where we are. It's like I'm holding my breath and waiting for the other shoe to drop.

While I want to believe that Jared and I have made it to the other side of our problems, and it'll be smoother sailing from here, a part of me knows that we haven't even gotten started.

Already, the rumor mill is buzzing, and while I do my best to avoid the gossip, in the dead of night, while Kayden is fast asleep and when Jared is not with us, I scroll the feed and read all the things being said about us.

Many of the comments are harmless, but a few leave me with a bad taste in my mouth.

I have been painted as a devious gold digger because of our age difference. Thankfully, Jared's PR team has managed to keep our personal information out of the tabloids, but we're living on borrowed time.

My only concern is for my family to find out. I'm sure I would get a call if they suspect anything. It seems as if they have not been exposed to the gossip yet.

With a slight shake of my head, I set my book down and stand up. I stretch my arms over my head and yawn. I glance over at Kayden and Jared, still bent over the coloring book and smile.

As I step into the kitchen with him, I feel Jared's eyes on me. I give him a small smile and he returns it, his entire face lighting up. His face breaks into a grin, and my heart skips a beat each time.

I lift the glass of water up to my lips and hide my smile.

Rebuilding the trust between us hasn't been easy, but it has been worth it. Jared and I have stealing moments for ourselves here and there whenever Kayden is asleep or at school, and I'm loving every minute of it.

The more time I spend with Jared, without any secrets between us, the more I remember why it was hard to let him go in the first place.

I don't want to be put in a position where I have to get over him.

Not again.

Once I'm done drinking water, I rinse my glass and wander back to the living room.

Kayden is nodding off, so Jared scoops him into his arms and carries him into his bedroom.

He sets Kayden down gently and pulls the covers up to his chin. Kayden stirs before falling into a deep and uneventful sleep.

Jared joins me in the doorway and drapes an arm over my shoulders. "Have I told you lately what a great mom you are?"

"It's been a few minutes," I tease, before pushing myself up on the tips of my toes. I give him a quick peck and draw back. "It can't hurt to hear it again."

Jared chuckles and steers me out of the hallway and into the living room. "In that case, I should tell you all the time."

I chuckle. "That might be overdoing it."

Jared and I lower ourselves onto the couch, and I snuggle against him, inhaling his musky scent. "You're doing a great job too by the way. Kayden is crazy about you."

Jared runs his fingers down the length of my back. "I feel like I'm messing up, but thanks."

I draw back and look at him. "I'm not just trying to butter you up, Jared. You really are doing great. I guess it helps that you've done it before, huh?"

Jared nods and pushes my hair out of my eyes. "Definitely. So, have you given any more thought to what I asked you the other day?"

I sit up and run a hand over my face. "Yeah, I don't know if I'm ready for us to go public."

"People are already speculating, and I don't want to keep you a secret," Jared replies, with a reassuring smile. "And I know things were bumpy last time, but you have nothing to worry about."

Except he and I both know it isn't true.

I still don't belong in his world and nothing is going to change that.

With a sigh, I rise to my feet and clear my throat. "One event, and we'll see."

Jared stands up and pulls me into a hug. "Great. There's a dinner tomorrow. Do you think Melanie and Cameron will be willing to babysit?"

"I'll check."

Jared draws back to look at me. "We can tell them whenever you're ready."

I nod. "I know."

·♥·♥·♥·♥·♥·

"You're sure it's okay? I know it's short notice." I hold the backpack out, and Melanie plucks it out of my hand. "Kayden's father has this big dinner thing, and since we're trying to give this a real shot, we can't stay in my apartment forever."

Melanie laughs. "Yeah, that's not how the world works. Soph, you know you can tell me anything, right?"

I shift from one foot to the other. "Yeah, I know."

Cameron waves at me in the background and swoops Kayden up. I glance back at Melanie who is lingering in the doorway, casting me a knowing look. "Someday, I hope you feel comfortable enough to tell me the truth about Kayden's father."

I swallow. "It's not that I don't want to. It's just been...complicated, and now that he's back in Kayden's life, I don't want to add any unnecessary complications."

Melanie waves my comment away. "You'll tell me when you're ready. Anyway, go and have fun. Call me later."

On my way down the stairs, I pause and listen for Kayden's laughter. When I step onto the sidewalk, Jared's car is waiting by the curb.

The uniformed driver holds the door open, and I get in, offering Jared a bright smile as I do. The drive to the other side of the city is quiet and contemplative.

I hold Jared's hand the entire way, trying to convince myself that I'm not making a mistake. As soon as we pull up outside a building with crowds of well-dressed men and women, my earlier fear returns.

Jared squeezes my hand and places a kiss on the inside of my wrist. "It's going to be okay. We've got this."

I give him an uncertain smile and allow him to lead me in. A loud cacophony of voices rises.

I stand up straighter, tuck my hand into the crook of Jared's elbow and let it wash over me. Inside the hotel, the ballroom is made of hardwood floors, with large windows overlooking the backyard, and a high arched ceiling.

Music is already filling the space, as is the smell of expensive perfume. Once Jared and I are noticed, we earn several curious looks.

A few people begin to whisper as we walk across to where Jared's business partners are standing on the other side of the room.

I feel their eyes on the back of my neck, judging and whispering, but I try to push it all away.

His business associates are a little more tactful, but I still feel their disapproval. I stay by Jared's side all night, allowing the conversation to drift over me. I savor the delicious food and how handsome Jared looks, knowing how much it all means to him.

Now and again, he squeezes my hand or presses a quick kiss to my cheeks, reminding me of why I'm doing this.

At the end of the night, when I duck into the bathroom stall and brace myself against the wall, I hear them.

I'm not sure if it's the same group of women, but through the slit in the door, I see them line up in front of the counter, dressed in their expensive dresses and stiletto heels, their faces covered in makeup.

"Can you believe he's dating her again?"

"She's gotten fatter."

"And did you see how thin and dry her hair looked? It's like she doesn't even own a mirror."

All three burst into laughter and exchange knowing looks. I push the stall door open and come out, my nails digging into the inside of my palms.

The three of them turn to me, their mouths half open and shocked looks on their faces.

"I know you must think you're really something," I begin, the blood roaring in my ears. "But having money doesn't make you better than other people. You might want to step away from the mirrors long enough to remember that."

Two of them sputter, and the third one, a tall blonde in a red dress, narrows her eyes at me. "We all know you don't belong here. Even you know that."

"Maybe, but I'm the one Jared comes home to every day," I reply evenly. With a saccharine smile, I pluck the champagne glass one of them left on the counter. "Enjoy your evening, ladies."

As soon as I step out, I lean against the wall and blow out a long breath. My heart is hammering as I down the drink and feel the smooth liquid descend.

I scan the crowd and see Jared standing nearby, one hand in the pocket of his suit, the other hanging limply at his side.

I hand the glass to a uniformed waiter with a tray and make my way to him. "What did I miss?"

Jared tucks me into his side and drapes an arm around my waist. "Not much. Everything good?"

I nod. "Yeah, don't worry."

This time I'm not going to take their jeers and derision lying down. I have every intention of giving Jared and me a fighting chance.

If it means having to go to bat for us, it's a price I'm willing to pay.

For the rest of the night, I stay by Jared's side, with my head held high and a smile plastered on my face. We earn curious looks and more than our fair share of disapproval, but I brace myself, using my love for Jared as a shield.

At the end of the night, as Jared and I stumble into the back of the car, I feel much better than I did hours ago.

Suddenly, facing off against the naysayers doesn't seem so hard. When Jared leans over to kiss me, smelling like whiskey and cologne, I link my fingers over his neck and sigh.

We can do this. Our love will overcome all these obstacles, and this will pass as everything else in life.

Chapter Twenty-One: Jared

"Stop that. Don't you have any manners at all?"

"You'd think his mother would've taught him better."

Sophie emerges red-faced, and her mouth pressed into a thin line.

She scoops Kayden up, gives them all a withering look, and looks over at me. "Can we talk in private, please?"

I offer my friend an apologetic smile. "I'll be right back."

Sophie holds Kayden to her and leads me into an empty room on the bottom floor.

Once the door clicks shut, she sets Kayden down on the bed and hands him a pair of headphones and her phone.

He props himself up against the pillow and focuses all of his attention on the device.

Sophie folds her arms over her chest and sighs. "Do they even know how to behave around a kid?"

"I'm sure they didn't mean to upset Kayden," I reply, with a shake of my head. "This is an adjustment for them, Soph."

Sophie shakes her head sharply. "No, an adjustment is them giving him too much candy or not knowing what kind of allergies he has. Yelling at my son in public is crossing a line."

"I don't know what you want me to do."

Sophie let her hands fall to her sides. "He's your son, Jared, and I'm....I don't know what I am, but I deserve to be treated better too."

"You're overreacting—"

"I am not overreacting," Sophie interrupts, with an incredulous look. "This is the second gathering we've been to where everyone whispers behind my back, takes digs at my job and my appearance and criticizes everything about Kayden."

I run a hand over my face. "It's not that bad."

A part of me knows she is right. I have done my best to shield Sophie and Kayden without rocking the boat, but I'm at my wit's end, and I have no idea what to do.

All I know is that Sophie and I are on opposite sides again, only this time I feel like if she walks away, there's no going back.

I can't lose her again.

"You and I both know that isn't true," Sophie tells me with a serious look. "We can't do this again, Jared. I won't let them do this to Kayden."

I take a step towards her. "I'm not going to let anything happen to Kayden, you know that."

Sophie searches my face. "Do you? Because I know you're trying to keep the peace, but sometimes you just have to say screw it and do what's right."

"It's my career, my business."

"And they're only treating me horribly because I'm not rich, and I don't run in the same social circles," Sophie replies, pausing to blow out a breath. "I want them to accept me, I want them to accept Kayden, but if this is the price we have to pay to be around them, then the answer is no."

"What do you mean no?"

"I mean, I'm not going to pay that price and neither is my son. They can go screw themselves for all I care."

I frown. "So, you're not even going to try?"

Sophie threw her hands up in the air. "I am trying. All I've been doing the past few weeks is trying to make myself smaller and try to make myself flashier and different just to please people I don't even like."

"I've been trying too."

"I know that, and you can't help that this is your world, but I can."

I freeze, lead settling in the pit of my stomach. "What are you saying?"

"We have to think about Kayden," Sophie tells me, after a lengthy pause. She glances over at him, still happily engrossed in his movie and looking impossibly small on the king-sized bed. "It's not just about us anymore."

"I know."

And I also know enough about Sophie as a mother to know that there is nothing she won't do for Kayden.

Including walking away from me again. The thought pains me, but I can't blame her for it.

For the longest time, it was just the two of them, and while I know that regardless of our relationship Sophie won't keep Kayden away from me, the thought of being separated hurts.

It weighs on me as we go back outside and re-join the party.

For the rest of the afternoon, I survey him; Sophie who bears it all with her head held high and a brave face.

I do my best to include her, but without support, I feel the walls are caving in around us...until we pile into my car at the end of the day, and I drive us back to the city.

Sophie keeps her face pressed against the glass the whole time while Kayden sleeps in the back.

When I reach between us for her hand, she shifts and angles herself so she's facing away from me. I try not to dwell on it.

Once we join city traffic and crawl forward at a snail's pace, she turns to face me. "I don't want to keep doing this, Jared."

I grip the steering wheel and spare her a quick look. "I know things are hard, but they won't always be."

Sophie sinks into her seat and rakes a finger through her hair. "Honestly, it doesn't feel like that right now. It just feels like we've fallen back into old habits."

And old problems. I grip the steering wheel tighter and press my lips together.

The rest of the ride is spent in silence. When I park the car in the underground garage, Sophie pushes her door open.

She carries Kayden in her arms and kicks the door shut with her leg. In silence, we take the stairs to the top floor and step out into the brusque night air.

As soon as we do, we are surrounded by paparazzi, on either side of the street, pointing their cameras and yelling.

Spots dance in my field of vision as I step closer to Sophie and hold an arm out in front of me.

Their voices grow louder, clamoring to be heard over each other. Sophie tucks Kayden between us, her face turning stony and expressionless.

We cross the street, with a great deal of pushing and yelling, and the doorman of my building sees us. He says something into his walkie-talkie and scrambles down the steps.

Once he reaches us, I push Sophie ahead of me and hurry after her. Together, we race up the stairs and away from the vultures, whose questions are growing more and more intrusive with each passing second.

When we are safely through the double doors, I escort Sophie to the elevator. I wait until she and Kayden are inside the apartment before I race downstairs, taking the stairs two at a time.

Once I reach the bottom floor, I am covered in sweat, and my breathing is heavy. I walk over to the main desk, lean over it, and slam my hands against the counter.

"How the hell did they end up outside?"

The uniformed man behind the desk jumps to his feet and links his fingers together. "Mr. Fox, we are so sorry. They've been here for hours, but they haven't actually done anything. We did place a call to the police, but when they were informed of the situation, they dismissed it."

I scowl. "I want them all gone. This is a private building."

The man's head bobs as he nods. "We'll do what we can, Mr. Fox. Is there anything you or Ms. Davenport need?"

"A time machine," I mutter underneath my breath. "Please get this taken care of as soon as possible."

Without waiting for a response, I take the elevator back up to my apartment. Once I step in through the door, I see Sophie lingering in the doorway to Kayden's room.

She has her arms folded over her chest and a strange look on her face. I let the front door click shut behind me, and I pause to lock it before walking over to her.

Sophie doesn't react when I stand next to her. "I'm sorry. I made sure they're going to take care of it."

Sophie sighs. "I know you've got connections, Jared, but even you can't keep us safe all the time."

I curl my hands into fists at my side. "It doesn't mean I won't try. Tomorrow, I'll look into hiring a security team for you and for me."

Sophie takes a step back and brushes past me. "So, this is what our life is going to be like now? Security teams and racing through people who all want to take pictures and print lies about us?"

I follow her into the kitchen. "It's part of the territory. You knew that already."

"I didn't sign up for this," Sophie mutters, pausing to swing the refrigerator door open. She pulls out a bottle of wine and pours herself a generous amount. "It wasn't this bad last time."

"They know about Kayden now, and I'm a private man," I reply, stopping to lean over the counter. "I know this is a lot to take in, but I need you to bear with me here. I will figure this out."

Sophie takes a long sip of her wine and sets it down with a little more force than warranted. "What if you can't, huh? I don't want Kayden to grow up like this,

Jared. Please don't look at me like that. It's not unreasonable for me to want our son to have a normal life."

I step out from behind the counter and hold an arm out. "It's not unreasonable, and I didn't say that it was."

Sophie sighs and steps into my arms. She searches my face, her expression troubled. "I don't want him to have those kinds of problems. He's not even four yet. He hasn't learned how to deal with any of this."

I drop my hands to her waist. "I know, but we'll learn to figure all of this out together. As a family. I just need you to not give up on us, okay?"

Sophie exhales. "I—"

I press a finger to her lips. "We don't have to talk about this tonight. Let's go take a shower and relax. Sleep on it, and we'll talk in the morning."

Sophie frowns. "Nothing is going to be different in the morning."

"No, but everything looks better after a good night's sleep, and a clearer head," I reply, with a small smile.

I step back and take her hand in mine. "How about I give you a massage?"

"Are you trying to butter me up?"

"That depends on whether or not it's working."

Sophie follows me into the bedroom and pulls her blouse over her head. "That depends on whether or not you throw in a glass of wine and a bowl of popcorn."

I kick off my shoes and lean forward to kiss her. "You've got yourself a deal."

When I move towards the door, Sophie hugs me from behind and presses her head against my back. "I don't want to give up on us."

I swallow and mutter, "Good. We've got this, don't worry."

She gives me another squeeze and pulls back. When I look over my shoulder at her, she is out of her clothes and stepping into the bathroom, butt naked.

I stare at her back for a few seconds before I twist the knob.

I stop and press my face against the door and exhale. I count backward from ten and wait for the knots in my stomach.

I have no idea what else I'm supposed to do.

Chapter Twenty-Two: Sophie

"Thanks for coming."

Melanie gives me a quick hug and steps back. She glances over my shoulders and waves at Kayden, who is sprawled on the floor, his toys spread in a circle around him. "Hi, buddy."

"Hi, Aunty Mel. Do you want to see my new toys?"

"Aunt Mel has to talk to mommy for a bit. She'll come and play with you when we're done, okay?"

"Okay," Kayden replies without looking up.

I take Melanie's hand and lead her to the terrace, where I put out two chairs and a table. I set a bottle of wine down in front of us, along with two glasses, and glance at her.

Melanie sets her purse on the floor and pushes her chair closer.

"Thanks for coming over so quickly," I tell her, pausing to pour us both a generous amount of wine. "I know I should've come clean years ago, but to be honest, I didn't see the point when we broke up."

Melanie reaches for her glass and takes a long sip. "This is about Kayden's dad, isn't it?"

I nod and swallow. "I want to tell you who he is."

Silence stretches between us. Between the paparazzi, the tabloid stories, and all of the contempt and derision at Jared's social circle's hands, I'm not sure I can handle anymore rejection.

Yet, I know that the time is right for me to tell Melanie. I don't want her to end up stumbling over the news in a magazine.

Or worse.

Still, I take a long sip of my wine and sit up straighter. "I don't know why this is so hard."

Melanie sets her drink down and takes both of my hands in hers. "Would it help if I told you that I know?"

I stare at her. "You can't possibly know."

Melanie's lips lift into a half smile. "we've known for a while. You and Jared are both careful not to talk about each other. You get this weird look on your face whenever his name comes up, and Cameron showed me a few pictures of his dad when he was younger. Kayden looks exactly like him. Your description of him and what we heard about him dating a younger woman, it all came together. Cam and I figured it out in the beginning. It wasn't really that hard."

I sag and grip her hands tighter. "Why didn't you tell me that you knew? You're mad, aren't you? Please don't be mad, Mel. I wanted to tell you, but I didn't know how to."

Melanie sighs and releases my hands. "Honestly, I was mad at first but then I realized you weren't trying to hurt me or Cameron. We just didn't say anything because we knew how hard it was for both of you to reveal your relationship. I'm sure the thought of being rejected by us wasn't easy.""

I take another long sip of my drink. "Neither of us were trying to hurt you. It just happened, and when things got serious enough that I wanted to tell you, we broke up."

Melanie nods. "I figured as much."

"Do you hate me?"

Melanie raises an eyebrow. "Why would I hate you? You fell in love.. these things happen. I'm not saying it's not weird that you fell in love with my father-in-law, but I guess stranger things have happened."

I set my drink down and throw my arms around Melanie. "You have no idea how much I needed to hear you say that, Mel. I've been so worried."

Melanie pats my back. "I know. I've just been waiting for you to realize that you were ready to tell me."

I squeeze my eyes shut. "You're amazing, Mel. I don't know what I did to deserve a sister like you."

Melanie laughs and pulls back to look at me. "I'm just glad you can finally be honest with me. I'm not sure it hasn't been easy for you. I've seen the tabloids."

I grimace and glance at Kayden, who hasn't moved from his spot. "He has no idea what's happening, and I have no idea how to protect him from this."

"You're a good mom, Soph. You'll figure something out. The more you try to control the situation, the worse it can get. Why don't you just relax about it and let things work its way out naturally? Jared won't let anyone hurt you or Kayden, trust him on this."

I swing my gaze back to Melanie and grimace. "Cameron hates me, doesn't he? Is that why he's been acting weird around me?"

"Cameron doesn't hate you. He is worried about you because he knows what his dad is like," Melanie replies, with a shake of her head. "He wasn't sure if Jared was serious about you or not, and he didn't want Kayden to get hurt."

"That's really sweet of him."

Melanie's expression turns solemn. "You two are serious, right? Because this is a lot of trouble to go through for a man."

"He's not just any man."

Melanie stands up and pours us both some more wine. "Yeah, I've known that from the minute I heard you talking about him, but I wanted to double-check. For Kayden's sake."

I nod. "Thank you. Kayden and I are lucky to have you and Cameron, of course."

"Cameron is with Jared now," Melanie tells me. "I think Jared is going to come clean to him and Olive."

I wince and pat my pocket. "I wonder why he didn't tell me. I would've been there to support him."

Melanie hands me my glass with a soft smile. "I think some things you just have to do on your own."

I frown. "Yeah, you're right. How do you think Mom and Dad are going to take it?"

Melanie shrugs and sits down. "I honestly have no idea, but we can find out if you want."

"Now?"

"No time like the present." Melanie stands back up and retrieves my laptop. My phone rings as she walks away, bringing me back to the present with a jolt.

I fish it out of my pocket, see Jared's name flash across the screen, and my heart skips a beat. With a smile, I step back into the apartment and bend down to ruffle Kayden's hair.

"Hey, are you on your way back already?"

"No, I've got something I need to do first. Can you turn on the TV?"

"I was going to call my parents and tell them," I reply, pausing to cradle the phone between my neck and shoulders. "Can this wait?"

"It's really important," Jared replies.

I point the remote at the TV above the mantel, and it comes to life. "Okay, what am I watching?"

"Turn to the channel nine news," Jared replies, his voice going muffled before it comes back on, clearer than before. "I'll call you back in a few minutes, okay? Don't switch off the TV."

I sit down on the couch, and Kayden comes to sit on my lap. When Melanie comes back into the living room, a laptop in hand, her brows furrowed together. "What's happening?"

"Ladies and gentlemen, thanks for coming out today." Jared appears on screen, in a crisp dark suit, with his hair slicked back and his children standing on either side of him. "I know we all have more important things to do, so I'll make this brief."

Several microphones are pointed at him, and everyone in attendance goes quiet. Jared stands up straighter against the company's building as a backdrop.

In the background, Olive and Cameron look extremely put together with their coiffed hair and ironed clothes.

Lead settles in the center of my stomach. What is Jared doing?

"There's been a lot of speculation recently about my personal life," Jared begins, pausing to squint into the distance. "I usually don't pay attention to any rumors or gossip about my personal life, but it's come to my attention that my son and girlfriend have been the target of these unsavory rumors."

A murmur rose through the crowd.

Melanie sits down next to me and drapes an arm over my shoulders. "Is he really…?"

I hold Kayden tighter and smile. "Kayden, look at your dad."

Kayden tilts to the side and squirms. "Why is he on TV?"

"Because your dad is a good man, and he wants the whole world to know how much he loves you," Melanie says without looking at him. She pats Kayden's hand and sits up straighter. "They're going to eat him alive, Soph."

"I know," I whisper, unable to look away from him.

He stands up straighter, his hazel eyes tight and focused. "As a businessman, I know that some of the attention comes with the territory, but I ask that you please respect the privacy of my son and his mother. Neither of them asked for any of this, and it's unfair to subject them to such behavior."

"Mr. Fox, is it true that she's half your age?"

"Is it true that your son is married to her sister?"

"What about the son? When do we get to see him?"

Jared holds a hand up and clears his throat. "This is a family matter, and I ask that you please respect our privacy during this time. Thank you."

With that, he spins on his heels, and his children close ranks around him. He pushes through the double doors of the building, and all of the reporters jump to their feet.

Chaos unfolds as everyone tries to talk at the same time, addressing their questions and concerns to a small blonde woman in sky-high heels, a bright smile plastered on her face.

When she steps onto the podium, I pick up the remote and switch the TV off.

Kayden jumps off of my lap and goes back to his toys. I pick up my phone and begin to pace. Jared answers on the fifth ring. "So, what did you think?"

"I think you're crazy. Why would you do something like that? Now, they're not going to stop hounding you."

"Better me than you," Jared replies, a smile in his voice. "And I told you I'd figure something out. I called a meeting with my team this morning, and we came up with the idea of a press conference."

I stop in the middle of the apartment and run a hand over my face. "I don't know what to say. This is the nicest thing anyone has ever done for me, Jared. It means a lot to me."

More than he will ever know.

"I had a Zoom session with the family this morning, and I told them all off."

I choke back a laugh. "You didn't, why?"

"Well, I was nice about it, or as nice as possible when you're telling someone to screw themselves when they give you a hard time about my relationship with you. I made it very clear that they need to treat you and Kayden with respect., or they would not see me again."

Tears fill my eyes. "You didn't have to do any of this."

"I did. I'm all in, Soph. I told you this already. You and Kayden are what's important to me, and I won't ever stop trying to prove that."

"I love you."

"Does this mean you approve of the press conference?"

I glance over my shoulders, at Melanie and Kayden playing together on the floor. "When you get home, I'll show you just how much I approve."

Jared's answering laugh was like music to my ears. "I love the sound of that, but it might have to wait."

"Why?"

The keys click in the door, and Jared steps in, his tie askew and with Olive and Cameron in tow. "We've got dinner guests."

I hang up and cover the distance between us. "Why didn't you tell me? I would've made something."

Jared takes me into his arms and kisses me. "I thought we could order something."

"I'm so glad I can finally welcome you into the family, officially, I mean," Cameron tells me, with a grin. "It's been hard keeping it from you."

I give Cameron a quick hug. "You did a good job."

Olive eyes me, carefully. "This is going to be an adjustment for all of us, but I think we can all agree to try to be a family."

I give Olive a warm smile. "I'd like that."

Olive blinks and glances over my shoulders. "Is that my brother?"

I step back and gesture to him. "Sweetheart, I want you to come over here and meet someone."

Melanie throws Kayden over her shoulders and carries him over while he squeals and giggles in delight. "Captain Mel reporting for duty with her right-hand man, Kayden."

She sets Kayden down on the floor, and he is bright-eyed and flush. "Hi, who are you?"

Jared drapes an arm over my shoulders and presses his mouth to my ear. "Wasn't I promised a token of your gratitude?"

I giggle and shove him away. "First, we eat, then we see. Kayden, why don't we go sit down on the couch?

Mommy has something very important she wants to tell you."

Chapter Twenty-Three: Jared

"Thanks for coming with me." I glance at Cameron in the mirror and smile. "I know we're all still getting used to things, but I'm sure this is what I want to do."

Cameron nods and lowers himself into the armchair. "It's your life, Dad. Personally, I wouldn't want to do it a second time. Marrying Melanie the first time was stressful enough. Not that I wouldn't do it all over again, but minus the wedding if I could."

I chuckle and nod to the tailor who steps back. "Being married to the right woman makes it all worth it."

Cameron looks up from his phone. "Sure."

I inch closer to him and shove both of my hands in my pocket. "Are you sure that you're okay with this?"

"I think Sophie is great, and the two of you deserve to be happy."

I stop in front of him and frown. "Why do I sense there's a but in there?"

"Olive is still trying to wrap her head around it," Cameron replies, with a grimace. He lifts his gaze up to mine and sighs. "It doesn't help that Mom has been filling her head with bullshit."

"Your mom will get over it."

Cameron stands up and brushes lint off of his collar. "Yeah, I know. I just wish she wouldn't turn everything into a soap opera, you know."

"She's still your mom, and this is hard for her."

She's not the only one who hasn't taken the news well.

Not only have I had to sit through several meetings with my board of directors and my PR team, all of them expressing concern over the public's perception of my relationship, but I've also had to work overtime to make sure my family stays in line.

Managing it all isn't easy. Thankfully, our numbers haven't suffered, and the media attention has slowed to something tolerable. Not that Sophie agrees.

Most days, it's hard to get her to go anywhere, much less with Kayden in tow. Little by little, she is coming out of her shell and embracing our life together though, and I couldn't be more thrilled.

All that's left is for me to make it official...the way I've wanted to for years.

"Is she giving you a hard time too?"

I shrug to say, "She'll come around. She just needs some time."

Cameron nods and brushes past me. "Sounds like you haven't told her about the proposal yet."

"I still have to ask Sophie to marry me, and she's got to say yes."

Cameron holds a tie up to the mirror. "She's definitely going to say yes, Dad. I've seen the way the two of you look at each other. I swear, I don't need to see the two of you making out."

I clap Cameron on the back and laugh. "You'll get used to it."

Cameron spins around and pulls a face. "I'd rather not. Anyway, what's the plan for tonight? You going out, or staying in?"

"Staying in. I've hired a chef to make us a nice dinner. There will be candlelight and music, and Kayden is going to help me propose."

Cameron raises an eyebrow. "How are you getting him to keep the secret?"

"It's cost me several candy bars, a raise in his allowance and increasing his bedtime by half an hour."

Cameron throws his head back and laughs. "Oh, man. He's got you good. Little dude's got skill. I like that."

"Yeah, he's giving me a run for my money. I think he might have the makings of a businessman."

Cameron shakes his head. "Don't go planning his future yet. There's still time. Why don't Melanie and I take Kayden off your hands for the night? After the proposal, I mean. Give the two of you a chance to celebrate."

"I appreciate the offer, but it's ok, I want him to be there."

"I'm really happy for you, Dad," Cameron offers. "And don't worry about Olive. She'll come around too."

·♥·♥·♥·♥·♥·

"Now?" Kayden glances over at Sophie, sitting out on the terrace in a black dress, her hair billowing behind her. "Mommy is going to love the ring."

I pat Kayden's head. "We're almost there, buddy. Do you remember what you're going to do?"

Kayden rocks back and forth on the balls of her feet. "Dad, you've already told me. I'm not a baby."

I crouch in front of Kayden and wait for him to meet my gaze. "I don't think you're a baby."

And I love that he's gotten into the habit of calling me dad. It was a little disconcerting at first, but now it's my favorite thing to hear. I can't believe how lucky I am.

I smile and hold my arms. Kayden steps into them, and I inhale the sweet smell of him, like baby shampoo and lemon scented soap. "You know that I love you, right, bud?"

Kayden nods. "I know, and I know you love Mommy."

I stir and draw back to look at him. "Mommy and I are going to love you no matter what happens between us, okay? I want you to understand that."

Kayden tilts his head to the side and looks at me. "What do you mean?"

"I mean, if Mommy says no, I am still your dad. I will always be your dad."

Kayden's lower lip juts out. "Why would mommy say no?"

"I don't think she will," I offer, with a bright smile. I stand back up and brush lint off of my collar.

In the kitchen, the bald-headed chef dressed in white with an apron tied around his waist is moving steadily, pausing only to issue instructions to his wait staff in clear and measured tones.

I want tonight to be perfect. But I suddenly wonder if I haven't done enough. I should've taken Sophie out to dinner somewhere nice and planned something more elaborate.

But I know Sophie, and how she prefers simplicity and hates all the pomp and circumstance. It's one of the many things I love about her.

The thought of proposing to her makes me start sweating all over again. I feel like a lovesick teenager on the eve of prom.

With a slight shake of my head, I tuck Kayden into my side and look over at the staff in my kitchen. "Chef Michael, how's everything going?"

"I need a few more minutes," Chef Michael replies, without looking at me. "You can't rush perfection."

I nod. "Of course not. Buddy, you sure you're going to be able to handle the tray?"

"Yes." Kayden lifts his head up and gives me a determined look. "I think Mommy is going to come in here. What do we do?"

"Act natural," I tell him, pausing to pat his head. When I wheel around to face Sophie, she takes my breath away, a vision in her black dress, her hair framing her face. "I'm sorry about all of this, Soph. I want to make sure everything is perfect."

Sophie raises an eyebrow. "I feel like the two of you are up to something."

Kayden clasps his hands behind his back. "We're not up to anything, Mommy."

Sophie's eyes narrow slightly. "Uh-uh. I'm going to pretend I believe you."

"Kayden is the one who made the salad," Chef Michael says, without looking over his shoulders. He stirs something on the stove and tastes it. "They wanted it to be a surprise, but I thought you should know. Your boy could become a chef someday."

Sophie's mouth splits into a grin. "Sweetheart, great job. I'm sure it's going to be delicious."

Kayden puffs his chest out. "I hope you like it, Mommy."

Sophie pulls him to her and tucks him into her side. "I'm sure I will. Do you want to watch a movie?"

Kayden glances at me and then back at her. "I'll play with my toys for a bit."

He darts off; moments later, his toys are clattering to the floor. With a grin, he lowers himself to the couch and makes whooshing noises with his car.

Sophie's smile is warm and tender when she looks at him. It makes me fall in love with her all over again.

I can't wait for us to be a family. I have no idea what I'm going to do if Sophie turns me down.

With a frown, I place my hand on the small of Sophie's back and lead her back onto the terrace, where a table has been set with a checkered tablecloth and two small candles in the center.

After pulling Sophie's chair out with a screech, I wait for her to sit and unbutton my jacket. I take a seat opposite her and reach for her hand across the table.

"What are you up to, Jared Fox?"

"I only have the worst of intentions," I tease, pausing to run my thumb along the inside of her wrist. "I just thought we needed a nice dinner together, and I wanted somewhere private."

Sophie snorts. "So, you turn your terrace and kitchen into a private restaurant? That's a little much, don't you think?"

"Not for you," I reply, with a smile. "I want you to have the full experience."

Sophie grins, and her entire face lights up. "Does this mean I can kick off my heels and play footsie with you under the table?"

"We can do whatever you want," I tell her, my eyes sweeping over her candlelight face, bathed in warm, buttery hues.

Underneath the moonlight, she is the most beautiful woman I've ever seen. My heart is going to jump out of my chest.

Why am I so nervous?

Sophie withdraws her hand and reaches for her drink. "I still can't believe you did that press conference without telling me."

I shrug. "I had a feeling you might try and stop me."

Sophie takes a long sip of her wine and smacks her lips. "Of course, I would've. I don't want your business to suffer because of me. You did mention that the board wouldn't be too happy with something like this."

"They'll get over it," I assure her, before reaching for my own drink. "And it hasn't affected our numbers. Public perception of me has changed, but the PR team thinks it might be a good thing. Something about a committed man bringing a level of respectability and authenticity to the brand."

Sophie sets her drink down and clears her throat. "So, in other words, now they think it's a good thing because it's driving up stock prices?"

"Something like that."

Sophie nibbles on a piece of garlic bread. "My parents are still freaking out."

"Do you want me to talk to them?"

Sophie tucks a lock of hair behind her ear. "No, I can handle it. They'll eventually get over it, once they get past the...unusual dynamic we have. Olive still giving you a hard time?"

"I'll manage."

Sophie sits up and brightens when a waiter in a black and white uniform emerges, carrying a tray with two soup bowls.

In silence, he sets them down and disappears. Sophie picks up her spoon, takes a long sip, and makes a low noise in the back of her throat.

"This is amazing. Where did you find this guy?"

"I helped him when he was starting out," I reply, in between sips of the thick, creamy mushroom soup. "He's in high demand and one of the best chefs in the city."

"Are you trying to impress me?"

I chuckle. "I thought I didn't have to do that anymore."

"You don't, but it sounds like you are."

"How are things going at the office?"

"The partners aren't too thrilled about my private life being thrust into the public eye, but for now at least, it doesn't seem like I'm going to be fired."

"They are not going to fire you."

"You don't know that."

"Want me to talk to them?"

Sophie makes a low strangled noise and dabs her mouth with a napkin. "No, that's going to make things worse. Besides, what do you think will happen if you try and talk to them?"

"They'll see the reason!"

Sophie chuckles and sets her napkin down. "They'll think I ran to you to complain because you're powerful and wealthy."

"I am powerful and wealthy."

Sophie makes a vague hand gesture. "That's beside the point. Anyway, I can handle it. If they want to fire me, I'm sure I can go and work somewhere else."

"You can come and work for me."

Sophie eyes me over the rim of her glass. "I know you don't need a real estate lawyer."

"I could."

Sophie throws her head back and laughs. "You're sweet, but no. I don't want people thinking I only got hired because I'm your girlfriend."

I swallow and pat my mouth dry. "You do realize people are going to say that anyway, right? I'm sorry that you have to deal with it, but it is part of the territory. It's what comes when you're dating a public figure."

"I know."

I set down my drink and clear my throat. "Are you sure? Soph, if this is too much for you…"

Sophie shakes her head and reaches for my hand from across the table. "I can handle it. You know you're not the only who's willing to fight for this relationship. I want this to work, Jared. I want our family."

Some of the knots in my stomach start to unfurl. "Good."

I twist in my seat and eye the chef through the sliding glass doors. A quick look passes between us before he looks away.

I spot Kayden hovering near the door, a toy in one hand and a piece of cake in the other. As soon as he sees me, he stuffs it into his mouth and gives me a sheepish look.

With a chuckle, I turn back around to face Sophie.

The blonde-haired waiter returns with two plates of steaming hot pasta, and the rich smell of cinnamon and ginger fills the air.

I pick up my fork and draw Sophie into a conversation. We talk and laugh while soft music plays.

When our plates are cleared, I sit back in my chair and study her.

Kayden comes out, carrying a tray of dessert. He carries the chocolate cake carefully, his bottom lip pooched out.

At the last second, he loses his balance and goes pitching forward.

The tray falls to the floor with a clatter, and Kayden lands face-first in the cake, sending splatters of food in every direction.

Sophie and I jump to our feet, but she gets to Kayden first, and I hold back.

"Are you okay? Don't worry about the cake."

Kayden nods, and his lower lip trembles. "I'm sorry, Mommy. I didn't mean to ruin dinner. Please don't be sad."

"It's okay, buddy. We can ask the chef to make another cake," I tell him, pausing to shoot the wait staff a look over my shoulders. "Why don't we get you cleaned up, okay?"

Kayden's face falls, and he lowers his head. "I'm sorry."

Sophie ruffles his hair and stands up. "It's okay. Accidents happen. Come on."

Kayden lifts his face to hers, and a furrow appears between his brows. "But it's not my fault. I tripped because I saw something shiny in the cake."

Sophie rises to her feet and frowns. "Something shiny?"

Kayden holds both arms out and opens his palm. "Look."

Sophie picks up a ring and holds it up to the light. "Are you sure you found this in the cake?"

I smile and lower myself onto my knee. "It looks good to me."

"What do you mean it looks good?" Sophie wheels around to face me, and her eyes widen. "Oh."

I hold my hand out, and she places the ring in my palm. "Sophie Davenport, I've loved you since the moment I stole your taxi outside the airport. I've loved you since you got into that taxi and refused to leave. I loved you even more when I saw you at your sister's wedding, and you realized who I was."

Sophie's breath hitches in her throat. "I love you too."

"I have been a better person because of you. You challenge me. You inspire me, and I love you more each day. I want this life with you and Kayden. I want us to be a family. Sophie, will you do me the honor of becoming my wife?"

Tears fill Sophie's eyes and spill down her cheeks. She lowers herself onto the floor and gives me a watery smile. "I can't wait to marry you, Jared Fox."

I grin and kiss her, soundly. When we pull apart for air, Kayden is cheering and jumping up and down.

He launches himself at us, and I hoist him up into the air and pull us all up for a hug.

The three of us sit at the table, with a third chair being added. Another cake is to be served.

"So, you guys planned all of this, huh? That's some pretty good planning."

"You fell for it, Mommy," Kayden said, in between bites of cake. He flashes her a smile full of chocolate icing. "Daddy told me a week ago, and I've been helping him plan everything."

"It's true. It was Kay's idea for me to hide the ring in the cake."

"And it was my idea to drop it," Kayden adds, with a proud smile. "You made a good decision, Mommy."

Sophie laughs and pats his hand. "I'm glad you think so, sweetheart because I think so too."

After dinner, the wait staff cleans everything up, and Sophie marches Kayden into the shower. Once she's done, I come into the room, and we tuck him into bed and read him a story.

We linger until his eyes grow heavy, and he falls asleep. At the doorway, Sophie hesitates and leaves the door propped open.

"I can't believe you pulled it off," Sophie whispers, bringing her head to rest against my shoulders. "How did you motivate him to keep it a secret?"

"Candy."

"That's it?" Sophie takes my hand and leads me into the bedroom. I shut the door and spin her around so her back is facing me. "There's got to be something else."

"I may or may not have promised him that he can get a raise in his allowance."

The dress pools at Sophie's feet, and she steps out of it in her bra and underwear. When she spins around to face me, her eyes are shining with humor and exasperation.

"I can't believe you bribed our son." Her fingers move over the buttons of my shirt till it falls to the floor with a flutter. "What am I going to do with you?"

"Oh, I should definitely be punished," I tell her, with a smirk. "You can do whatever you want to me."

Sophie steps back and points at the bed. "Start by taking all of your clothes off and getting onto the bed."

I touch two fingers to my brow and give her a salute. "Yes, ma'am."

Sophie saunters over to me, an intoxicating vision. She stops at the foot of the bed and twists her arms behind her back.

Her bra falls to the floor with a flutter, revealing her majestic breasts.

She gives me a smile, through hooded lashes, and hooks a thumb through the elastic of her panties.

My mouth is watering as I watch her get rid of the last piece of clothing. She climbs onto the bed, and my hands move to her waist.

She pins them over my head and rubs herself against me. "It's my turn."

I wriggle against her. "We can both have our fun."

Sophie lowers her head to kiss me, tasting delicious. "We will. Kayden is exhausted, and he's going to be asleep for a while."

I nip on her lower lip. "Maybe we should invest in a soundproof room."

Sophie throws her head back and laughs. "I like the way you think, Mr. Fox. How do you want me?"

She releases my hands, and they move to the curve of her hips. "I want you everywhere."

Sophie's lips lift into another seductive smile that has the blood roaring in my ears. "Good answer."

When she sinks onto me, taking me completely inside of her, I dig my nails into her flesh and take one nipple between my teeth.

She throws her head back and begins to bounce up and down, her moans reverberating inside of my head. I wonder if I'll ever get used to them.

As soon as I move onto the other nipple, Sophie turns frantic, raking her fingers down my chest and over my arms. Her eyes open, she looks directly at me, and I am falling.

But I know she's going to catch me. No matter what. For some reason our love making is getting better and better each time. We lose ourselves in each other in a unified sacred dance.

We become a single body and I can't distinguish who's guiding the motion or where it originates, as we both move together in the most mesmerizing synchronic dance.

How is that even possible?

Chapter Twenty-Four: Sophie

"How do you feel?"

"Like I'm going to be sick." I place a hand over my stomach and move away from the mirror. Melanie is standing behind me in a knee-length lilac dress, her hair piled on the top of her head.

She steps forward to help me with my dress, the loud rustling sound reverberating inside my head. Slowly, I lower myself onto the armchair by the window overlooking the hotel's backyard.

The guests are already pouring in, smart-looking in their suits and fancy dresses.

I fan myself and blow out a breath. "Maybe agreeing to a wedding was a bad idea. Do you think it's too late to call it off?"

Melanie sits down opposite me. "You can if you really want to, but I'm pretty sure you're going to piss off a lot of people and have a lot of tongues wagging."

I sigh and stare at the ceiling. "Now I know how Julia Roberts' character felt in *Runaway Bride*."

Melanie chuckles. "You're not going to pull a Julia, are you?"

I shake my head and look at Melanie, who is leaning back in her chair, one leg crossed over the other. "No, but I don't know if I can go out there and face all of those people. They're already judging me and wondering how I tricked the Jared Fox into marriage."

Melanie puts down her bottle of water and snorts. "Do you care what they think? They're going to be talking about you anyway. You and I both know that. Why do you even care about what they say? They move to the next gossip in a heartbeat when something juicier surfaces. Sis, you shouldn't care about what others think of you. It's important what you think of yourself and how you perceive yourself; then you radiate that energy. If you're confident then everyone sees you as confident. If you feel scared and worry about what people think of you, then everyone sees you as this timid person who's constantly seeking other people's approval, and they start to treat you that way. So, sis, I love you, but it's time to let go of all those thoughts and feelings you have about what they think about you and focus on yourself and just raise your confidence and it'll get better. I promise you that."

"WOW! How did you get so wise? I'm impressed how my little sis is so right in so many ways. Thank you! I needed to hear that."

Melanie leans forward and pats my hand. "My pleasure...anytime....anything for my love."

"I love you too! Where's Cameron?"

"He's with Jared now. So is Olive."

I blink, a half-smile on my lips. "At least she's coming around. Any news about their mom?"

"Olive claims she's boycotting the event, but I don't trust her not to do something."

My stomach twists. "Like what?"

"I don't know, but you best believe I will body slam her if she goes anywhere near you," Melanie assures me, with a lift of her chin. "I may not be able to stop her from coming in, but I sure as hell won't let her get anywhere near you."

"She's not actually going to try anything, is she?"

Melanie hesitates and runs a hand over her face. "Olive can be great, but she can also be a little intense. I think she's more bothered by the idea of you than the actual you. Cameron thinks she was hoping to get a little more money out of his dad."

I frown. "I'm sorry."

Melanie shrugs. "Welcome to the family, sis."

I sit up straighter and clear my throat. "Have you spoken to Mom and Dad?"

Melanie's face falls. "I've tried, but I don't know if they're coming. I just think it's a little too much for them right now. It's not that they don't want to support you."

I stand up and wander over to the mirror. I stare at my reflection, noting the elaborate updo that leaves a few wisps of hair to frame my face.

My eyes lined with kohl are enhanced with a smokey eyeshadow, giving me a sultry look. With a frown, I shift closer to the mirror and touch the glass.

"You'd tell me if you thought I was making a mistake, right?"

In the glass, I see Melanie stand up and walk over to me. "Sis, you know I would. I wouldn't let you go through with this if I didn't think you were making the right call. You love Jared, and he loves you...and you both love Kayden. There's nothing wrong with wanting to be a family."

I spin around to face her and sniffle. "I didn't mean to fall in love with him. I know it's a weird situation because I'll be your sister and your stepmother-in-law...."

Melanie pulls a face. "Don't remind me, I've been trying to forget."

"Stop trying to make me laugh."

Melanie takes both of my hands in hers and squeezes them. "I won't, but look, is it weird that we're going to become relatives in more ways than one? Yes. Will I get over it? Probably. The only thing I care about is your happiness. That's all that matters."

I give her a small smile. "I wish Mom and Dad felt the same."

Melanie pats my hand. "They will. It'll just take time."

With that, her face turns green and she darts into the next room, to the bathroom. She stumbles on the tile floor, holds her head over the toilet and empties her stomach.

I follow her, hold her head up, and use my other hand to rub her back.

"Okay, this is the second time you've thrown up today. Is everything okay?"

Melanie uses a paper towel to wipe her face. She pushes herself up to her feet and stands in front of the sink. After rinsing her mouth, she holds my gaze in the mirror and exhales.

"I wanted to tell you after the wedding because I wanted this day to be about you—"

I squeal and pull her in for a hug. "Mel, oh my God. Why didn't you tell me sooner? I'm so happy for you. You and Cameron are going to make amazing parents, and I know you've been trying for a while."

"I can't believe it's finally happening," Melanie whispers, into my ear. "This is not how I planned to tell you by the way."

I give her a firm squeeze and pull back. "I don't care. I'm just happy you told me. I can't wait to be an aunt. I'm going to spoil them rotten."

In between giggles, we step back into the room so I can help Melanie fix her makeup. Someone knocks on the door, and Melanie adjusts my dress.

She picks up her bouquet, flashes me a winning smile and hovers in the doorway.

"See you out there, sis," she says, over her shoulder. She's gliding down the stairs, a vision in her lilac dress, while I wait at the top.

When I hear familiar music, I climb down and clutch the bouquet of flowers in my hand.

I can't shake the feeling that something is missing. It isn't until I reach the bottom of the stairs and adjust my dress that I realize what it is.

None of this feels right without my parents, but I can't make them be here. Nor can I make them accept any of this.

Instead, I hold my head and walk through the brightly lit hallway, with streamers and colorful balloons everywhere.

As soon as I step outside, the sun is directly in my eyes, and I flinch.

When my vision clears, I see the chairs lined up on either side of the aisle, flowers strewn down the path, and an archway made of an array of roses, where Jared and the priest are waiting.

My eyes land on Jared, and when my vision clears, I hear sharp intake of breath. It's mine. In his dark, custom-made suit and a button-down shirt, he takes my breath away.

Once he smiles, my heart starts beating faster, and the music starts washing over me.

I take one step forward and another, beaming, when I spot Kayden next to his dad in a matching suit, waving enthusiastically.

Next to him, Cameron and Olive stand with their backs erect and heads held high.

I am halfway down the aisle when the screech of tires fills the air. My parents come in, racing, red-faced and out of breath.

Melanie gestures to the front pew, where a few empty seats await. Mom takes hers.

When my father adjusts my veil and tucks my hand into the crook of his elbow, a lump rises in the back of my throat. "I wasn't sure you were going to come."

"We weren't sure either, but we knew that regardless of how we feel about your choices, we couldn't miss your wedding."

I emit a sniffle. "Thank you for coming."

He falls into step beside me, and we glide down the aisle. Before he gives me away, he pauses to push my veil back and presses a kiss on my cheek.

Mom pulls me in for a hug and squeezes my shoulders. My heart is full and pounding against my chest. When Jared takes my arm, I come to a stand next to him.

I glance over at Melanie, busy dabbing her eyes. She offers me a watery smile. I look over at Kayden then back at Jared and smile widely.

I take both of his hands in mine and look into his eyes while the priest talks. All our friends and family are scattered throughout the pews, watching us, hanging on our every word.

All I can see is Jared's smile and the devious smirk hovering on the edge of his lips. As we stand beneath the setting sun, I can't wait to marry him.

Everything we've been through over the past few years has to led to this moment - standing underneath the arch and about to be joined in holy matrimony.

When Kayden begins to shift and fidget, the priest gives him an indulgent smile, and he stands up straight.

Cameron holds out his father's ring, and Melanie does the same with mine. A tremor shoots through me when I slide Jared's ring onto his finger.

With steady and sure hands, he takes my hand in his. I marvel at how he feels as he slides the ring on my finger. Once we're done, Jared places an arm around my waist and pulls me closer.

"I now pronounce you man and wife. You may kiss the bride."

"Fucking finally," Jared mutters, with an apologetic look in the priest's direction. "Sorry, Father."

The priest waves his comment away. Jared is drawing me into his arms and kissing me like my life depends on it.

I melt into his arms and cling to him for dear life, the rest of the world melting away.

The butterflies in my stomach start to dance, and my toes curl. When he draws back to look at me, with that same beautiful smile etched onto his face, I am breathless.

Little by little, I notice the thunderous applause punctuated by cheers and whistles. Kayden throws his arms around both of us and giggles.

Jared laces his fingers through mine and leads me through the pews to the makeshift dance floor set up in the backyard, with rows of trees on either side.

Slowly, the applause dies down and the band begins to play, the soft strings of a violin filling the air. I link my fingers around Jared's neck as he wraps his arms around my waist.

With a smile, I glance over at Kayden and see him dancing with Melanie, Cameron and Olive, a bright smile on his face.

Out of the corner of my eye, I see my parents drift onto the dance floor; it makes the swell of emotion in my chest grow further. With a sigh, I look back at Jared and inch closer so there's no space between us...as if I could climb inside his skin and stay there.

"What's on your mind?" Jared spins me out and back into his arms. "Let me guess, you're thinking about our wedding night."

I laugh when he dips me back and hoists me up. "I wasn't thinking about our wedding night. I'm just really happy my parents came."

Jared clears his throat. "Don't get mad, but I talked to them."

"What?"

"I knew how unhappy you were that they weren't coming. I told them how much it would mean to you, and how happy you would be. I also told them that you deserve the world and I was sorry it had taken me this long to realize it. Are you pissed?"

I push myself up on the tips of my toes and kiss him. "Thank you. That's one of the nicest things anyone's ever done for me."

Jared smiles into the kiss. "I'm glad you're not pissed, but I have to admit I was looking forward to the makeup sex."

I slide back and pinch his arm. "Who says we can't do it anyway?"

Jared chuckles as we move across the dance floor, oblivious to the world around us. "I like the way you think, Mrs. Fox."

"Who says I'm taking your last name? I happen to like my name just fine, thank you very much."

Jared chuckles. "How about a hyphen?"

"I'll think about it," I tease, pausing to place my head in the crook of his neck. "You know who you married."

He smells like old spice and soap.

"I do, and I'm glad that I finally came to my senses. It took a few years, but at least we finally made it."

"That's true."

"So... about the honeymoon, I know you told me you don't care, so here's what I was thinking. You and I fly to Bali for a few days, and from there, we meet up with everyone in Paris."

I look at him, a furrow between my brows. "Everyone?"

"Kayden, Melanie, Cameron, Olive, and your parents are all going to be on a family vacation in Paris. Kayden can enjoy Disneyland Paris till we catch up with them. This way, I get you all to myself for a few days before we join the family trip."

My stomach dips, and a familiar fluttering starts. "You're amazing. Have I told you that lately?"

Jared taps his chin. "You know I can't remember, so just in case, you should probably keep telling me."

I throw my head back and laugh. "Someone is getting a big head."

"Guilty as charged. There's nothing to be done about that."

I lower my head and stare at him through fluttering lashes. "I can think of a few suggestions."

The sun begins to dip below the horizon, bathing the world in hues of pink and purple. A cold breeze wafts past, carrying the scent of freshly cut grass and wildflowers.

Jared is smiling when he presses his mouth to my ear and whispers, causing a flush to rise up my neck and stain my cheeks.

When I pull back to look at him, I am grinning and wondering how I ever got so lucky.

With my family by my side, what more could I possibly need in this life?

THE END

Chapter Twenty-Five: Sneak Peek

I hope you enjoyed "My Secret Baby With The Billionaire"

Here is a sneak peek of Olivia's newest book:

"A Heated Rivalry With Baby Daddy: A Grumpy Off Limits Age Gap Romance" https://books2read.com/u/31BJkr Universal Link

https://www.amazon.com/dp/B0CVWYJSLH

Reviews:

Man, when you read this book about Ella and James you are going to feel like you are in Las Vegas playing the slot machines and just hit the JACKPOT. This book by Olivia has LOVE written all over it and once you start to indulge yourself into reading this book you won't want to pull away because it will grab onto you tightly and not let go. I can't say enough good things about how Olivia writes a steamy and oh so romantic book. So, look out because this book right here is going to be a best seller and a must-read book. (Review on Amazon)

this book was absolutely fantastic and will definitely have you hooked from the beginning until the end. Ella and James work in the same building and use same elevator but both don't talk to each other until the elevator stops and power goes out and he keeps her calm but before they get rescue they grab each other's work. This book is absolutely compelling and captivating and tantalizing and so much more. You will definitely fall in love with these characters. (Review on Amazon)

I really enjoyed this book. The build up of the relationship was great with lots of romance and excitement. (Review on Amazon)

Blurbs:

An elevator ride with a sizzling hot masked stranger became my morning ritual that made my day, but I didn't expect him to make my baby

too.

Mysterious and captivating, he ignites a flutter in my heart; his hidden features become the subject of my infatuation.

But his cold and anti-social demeanor gives me a knot in my stomach.

Our worlds collide with an unexpected breathtaking kiss, igniting a chain of events.

I just happened to find out that he is my boss' worst nightmare and an old rival.

No one is clear about their relationship, but one thing is clear, we are to steer away from each other.

He's my rival, and he is off limits; nothing good would ever come out of this.

Our strong burning chemistry for each other doesn't understand the language of logic.

uage of logic.

I want him and he wants me, it's that simple.

So, we have rules to do each other and to do work; do not mix them together, and no one should find out.

It definitely didn't go as planned.
Everything went down and ugly, and I am left all alone with a baby.

Content Warning: This book includes spicy content. Reader discretion is advised.

A Heated Rivalry With Baby Daddy: A Grumpy Off Limits Age Gap Romance

Chapter One: Ella

The masked stranger is getting into the elevator again.

"Hold it," I shout as I run down the hallway, coffee secured in my hand. "Hold it!"

I almost skid over the polished woodwork and rethink my 7 am decision to wear heels.

I see the doors slide open, and the masked stranger looks my way. Something electric courses through me as our gazes meet.

There is something chaotic about him today, compared to his usually calm exterior. I've seen this man several times a week for the past couple of months.

I've never heard him utter a word. I feel drawn to him for reasons I cannot explain.

He steps into the elevator and doesn't hold it for me. Then the door slides shut.

"Damn it," I curse under my breath. I check my watch. I'm seven minutes late, and by the time I swipe in my ID card, I'll be eleven minutes late.

The other elevator is out of order, as it has been for the past week. All the other wings in the Tech Park have at least four elevators, but we have only two.

Of course, I could just head to the east wing, and take the long route to my office but it's too much work—especially in my Mary Janes.

Just as I'm thinking this, the elevator doors open again. What's it doing down here so quickly? I step inside.

I blink in shock. The masked stranger is nowhere to be seen.

The masked stranger. That's what I call him in my head. I see him in the elevator several times a week. I've no idea where he works.

There are several companies and start-ups operating out of the Tech Park. All I know is that, but he gets off on one of the floors above mine.

I press the button to the tenth floor. Music plays somewhere overhead, a catchy pop song.

I wonder if there's secretly a DJ who comes in every morning to pick out the songs.

I sprint out of the elevator as soon as it reaches my floor. I have to walk past a couple of offices before I can get to SpringWeather Tech where I work.

SpringWeather Tech is the brainchild of our CEO, Allen Groves, who conceived it right out of college.

Thanks to a generous donation from his parents and an unused warehouse owned by his family, Allen was able to start a company that reached a valuation of five million in its very first year.

Impressive!

But he's not the dragon I need to slay this morning.

No, that would be Raine.

She leans against a desk by the door while she sips on coffee.

My coffee has already grown cold, and honestly, after facing such betrayal by the masked stranger, I don't want to drink it either.

"Ella," Raine greets me. She has a strained smile on her face. "You're late. Again."

"Good morning to you, as well, Raine," I chirp as I swipe my ID card, clocking myself in.

She narrows her eyes at me. "We had a meeting scheduled. I sent you a reminder."

By that, she means the multiple reminders and notices that she put on my Google and Zoom calendars so that anytime I opened my phone or computer, the notice jumped out at me.

"I got the reminder the first time you sent it," I tell her.

"And yet you didn't bother replying."

"I did reply," I say. "The first two times."

Raine narrows her eyes at me. "Well, we have a problem."

"What problem?" I ask.

"Let's go to my office and talk," she says.

That doesn't sound good.

We walk past the cubicles that are given to the lowest employees in the hierarchy—the interns.

My cubicle is on the north wing of the floor, far away from Raine's prying gaze. We're free to decorate our desks as we please.

I walk past one workspace dedicated to Jurassic Park and another to Star Wars. Is it obvious yet that I work with nerds?

I flip my hair behind me. A few people gawk at me, and I know why they're looking.

About forty people work here, and I'm the only female developer on the team. But that's not the reason I stick out like a sore thumb.

"We've discussed our outfits before, yes?" Raine says, launching into her no-nonsense tone as soon as we step inside her office. By our, she means mine.

I look down at myself. I'm wearing a bubble-gum pink cardigan, a sensible pencil skirt that brushes my knees, and matching pink accessories.

"As you suggested, I've toned down the pink," I say. "And I don't remember there being a formal dress code in our contract."

Allen is not in the office most of the times, so it's not like he cares.

"I can see that. And yes, you're right about there being nothing about this in the contract," Raine says, her lips pursed.

Her tone gives me the impression that she doesn't see anything at all.

I won't be surprised if she tracked Allen down today and begged him to put it in. "I was thinking of more work-appropriate clothes. As you know, there's a lot of men around here."

Jesus Christ, is that all there is to it?

I raise a brow at her. Is she serious right now? "And?"

She huffs in frustration. I totally understand where she's going with this, but I need her to be clear.

"You need to tone it down, ma'am," she says.

I don't know what her problem is. Just because she comes to work looking like she came straight from interviewing the devil doesn't mean I have to.

"Is that all?"

She forces a smile. "These are only suggestions."

"Of course," I say. "I hope you suggested the same to Josh when he came wearing his 'Incel Inside' shirt."

With the Incel written like Intel, it's supposed to be a funny pun or whatever.

Raine sighs. "Yes, I did speak to him." But I notice that she scribbles something in her notebook, like a reminder for herself.

"I just wanted to say that I want the best for everyone. As your HR person, I'm here to protect you."

"I get it," I say.

I don't even bother taking a seat as I exit her office. I know what people think of me when they see me, but I'm not about to change.

"Oh, and Ella?" Raine calls out from behind me. "You have a meeting with Allen tomorrow."

It's bad news, it has to be. Allen hardly ever makes an appearance at the office. He's mostly busy in Paris, strutting his new girlfriend.

I swallow hard. "I'll be there."

· ♥ · ♥ · ♥ · ♥ · ♥ ·

The next day, I step into the elevator, the same one I ride every morning, to reach my office on the tenth floor.

I'm sweating my skin off as I think of my impending meeting with the CEO.

I've only met him once when I was first hired. And the only thing he said to me was, "You really love pink, huh?"

Distracted, I press the button to my floor and lean back against the wall.

As the doors slide shut, I realize I'm riding with *him* again today. The masked stranger.

My heart skips a beat, even though riding with him has been almost routine this past few months.

He obviously doesn't notice me the way I notice him. This needs to change, too. But I try to get past that.

He's my crush. I don't need to know anything more to daydream about him.

As usual, he wears a face mask, making it impossible to see anything but the top half of his face. There's something about him that intrigues me.

The only two other people who were in the elevator leave when the elevator stops at their floor.

Now, it's just us riding the elevator together.

There's an air of mystery surrounding him, and I find myself stealing glances whenever we share this brief journey together.

He has dark brown hair that is immaculately combed back and every strand of hair is perfectly in place, giving him a polished and refined look.

His nose disappears inside the mask. He doesn't even glance my way, but I have seen his eyes before. I have looked into his eyes in the elevator many times.

They are mysterious like a dark deep blue ocean.

I only found out his name—James—because somebody who got in with us called him by that name.

Even then, I had my doubts because he didn't acknowledge that name or that person, who, in turn, looked miffed.

Does this mean he's just a loner who likes to keep to himself or one of those wannabe tech bros that want to appear brooding and mysterious?

I honestly hope he's not a tech guy because the men in tech here are insufferable. I know firsthand because I work with them.

I have an urge to pull down his mask and see the rest of his face. I've often fantasized about what's underneath.

I don't see a hint of a beard creeping up the side, but that doesn't mean he doesn't have stubble.

I've spent hours when I don't have anything better to do doodling what his face might be like underneath the mask.

Safe to say, I'm obsessed with him in a way that even I don't understand.

I stare ahead, thinking about my impending meeting with Allen.

I was so nervous this morning that I didn't even get my usual cup of coffee from my favorite indie café down the block.

But running into him here today makes me feel a little better, and I try to push past whatever happened yesterday when he didn't hold the elevator for me.

Somehow, being in this enclosed space with the stranger feels oddly comforting—a reminder that we are all individuals navigating our own journeys, each with our own fears and uncertainties.

I steal a quick glance at him, hoping to find a sense of calm mirrored in his eyes.

His gaze meets mine briefly, and even though he knows nothing about my life or me, it fills me with reassurance.

We exchange no words during our elevator rides. I find myself looking forward to these moments—these fleeting encounters in the confined space of the elevator.

I get my courage just as the doors open to my floor.

"Hey," I call out weakly. "Thanks for trying to hold the door yesterday."

He turns his body towards me slightly before walking out without even acknowledging my words.

Great, my first words to him, and I must have come off as a total psycho.

To my surprise, Allen is standing outside. "Ella, is it?"

I blink at him in shock. Is he here for me?

"Yes?" I say.

"Right on time," he says, nodding at me. Right on time for what?

I spare a glance at the stranger who is busy on his phone, AirPods plugged into his ears.

"Follow me," Allen says impatiently.

"Okay," I say, hopping out of the elevator. He starts to walk briskly ahead, as if he's in some kind of power-walk marathon.

"Walk with me," he says. I'm still confused about where he's going with this.

"I need to get in ten-thousand steps today," Allen explains. "I made a stupid bet with a friend and if I don't win, he gets my yacht."

This is more information that I've gotten about Allen in the eight months I've been working at this office. It makes sense.

Tech billionaires are eccentric. Or at least that's one of the few nicer words I can think of.

"So what did you want to talk about?" I ask.

"Are you aware of a little incident that took place last week concerning Devan Willborough," he says.

"Not exactly," I say. I've heard bits and pieces, and Raine pretty much tried to suppress it.

"I know that he tried to take off the wig of a girl in a subway." According to Devan, he was drunk and on his way home when he came up with this plan.

"Not a girl, a drag performer," Allen says. "And one with a lot of followers on social media. They're now suing Devan."

"Oh my God," I say, clapping a hand to my mouth. I had no idea it had become a big deal.

When I first heard about it, they were saying that it was Devan's hair being pulled out.

"I personally think it's no big deal, and has no grounds," Allen continues.

"But recently, our company has been tagged in a lot of Twitter and LinkedIn posts. We have to suspend Devan for a few weeks, maybe even let him go."

"Oh no," I say.

Allen's face pinches. "That's the last thing I want to do, but I don't have much choice. People won't stop with him. Social media can be quite vicious. The last thing I need is for it to drag Spring down."

"Yeah, no," I say.

Allen stops walks. "Are you with me?"

The intensity of his question catches me off-guard. "I'm sorry what?"

Allen rolls his eyes good-naturedly. "I'm sorry, I often don't remember that people don't think the same way I do."

I think it's supposed to be an insult but I ignore him.

"Sooo..." I trail off.

"Right, right, as I was saying, Spring has recently reached the glorious ten-year mark; however, we aren't turning over profit at the same rate as we were three years ago."

"Before the pandemic," I say.

Allen doesn't say anything, and I can tell I misspoke.

"That's mostly because of all the chatter happening in the AI-sphere," he says.

By that, he probably means ChatGPT. Only someone like Allen can refer to ChatGPT as mere chatter. "Now is the time to stand out."

My heart begins to beat fast. "And?"

"There's a prestigious network conference happening in Boston two months from now. Eighteen startups and firms have been invited to showcase the best of their brilliant new minds. The winner gets a billion-dollar contract from Yoros."

I gasp at the name. Yoros is *the* company to work at if you want to be someone as a developer or a cloud architect.

Only the best from ivy league colleges are picked, not that it stopped me from applying. I wasn't even invited for an interview.

"We're going to be working with Yoros?" I say. I can hardly believe it.

Allen's face tells me this is exactly the reaction he was hoping for. "Yes. It will be a five-year contract. SpringWeather will reach heights that we could previously only dream of. And you're the only person who can help me."

The music in my head stops playing as I yank out of my maladaptive daydream. "I'm sorry what?"

"Devan had been working on the project," Allen says. "Unfortunately, he has to drop out, which means we'll need a new face for it. And what better face than yours? Our newest and youngest hire, who also happens to be a woman"

"Okay," I say, amazed that he even knows who I am. This can't be a coincidence.

Allen must have gone through the painstaking process of sifting through numerous employees before he finally settled on me.

And then his motivation finally dawns on me—he intends to use me to fix the damage that dumbass Devan caused.

"You'll obviously have a dedicated team. I've already instructed David, Arjun, and Ian. You'll be taken care of."

"What exactly will our role be in this competition?" I inquire, my voice steady despite the underlying excitement.

"We'll be developing a cutting-edge application that addresses a specific industry challenge," Allen explains.

He continues, "Our goal is to not only provide a superior solution but also to showcase our innovative approach and technological expertise."

As Allen describes the vision and scope of the project, I feel a surge of energy building within me.

The opportunity to create something ground-breaking and impactful fills me with a renewed sense of purpose.

"I believe in our team's potential," Allen concludes. "I know we can rise to this challenge and make a name for ourselves. Are you up for it, Ella?"

His question catches me off-guard. "I—" I begin.

The look on his face tells me that saying no is not an option.

If I refuse, he might fire me and replace me. It won't be hard to find a blonde who loves to code, I guess.

"I would love to take it on," I say.

Allen nods, satisfied. "I expected nothing less."

He stops walking and presses a few buttons on his smartwatch.

A few minutes later, Raine approaches us with a file in her hands.

She hands it over to Allen, and she looks less than pleased when she sees me standing beside him.

Allen hands the file over to me. "This is all the progress Devan made. Look it over, and tell me what you think of it. I'm off to Miami in a few days. We'll talk when I get back."

"Sounds like a good idea," I say.

Raine turns to me, her lips pursed. "So, you got the project, huh?"

"Yep," I say. I get the feeling she hates me, and I still don't understand why. I've been nothing but nice to her.

I'm still wrapping my head around everything when the work day ends, and I clock out and head towards the elevator.

I took a look at the file earlier, skimming through the content. Devan might be an ass, but he's also a pretty smart coder.

It will be difficult to fill his shoes. And what if I come up short?

As I step into the elevator, I'm startled to see the stranger already inside.

The doors close, enveloping us in silence, and I try to shake off the residual excitement from my meeting.

Before I can fully process his presence, the lights abruptly flicker and then go out, casting the small space into complete darkness.

Panic seizes me, and I feel my heart race in my chest.

My initial instinct is to freeze, but the darkness overwhelms my senses, leaving me disoriented and vulnerable.

I scream and blindly stumble forward. Without thinking, I shoot my arms out, seeking something solid to hold onto. And in that moment, I find myself stumbling into the stranger's arms.

It's a reflex, an instinctual move to seek comfort and reassurance.

My body trembles, a mixture of fear and adrenaline coursing through me.

I can feel his strong arms encircling me, providing a sense of stability in the darkness.

Continue to read for FREE on Kindle Unlimited:

https://books2read.com/u/31BJkr Universal Link to Amazon site

https://www.amazon.com/dp/B0CVWYJSL

· ♥ · ♥ · ♥ · ♥ · ♥ ·

Here is a sneak peek of another book:

"Surprise Babies For My Billionaire Rancher: A Mistaken Identity Vacation Romance"

https://www.amazon.com/dp/B0CQX25K9 Direct Amazon Link

https://books2read.com/u/4Aazzq Universal Link to Amazon

Reviews:

I really enjoyed reading Surprise Babies for My Billionaire Rancher! Danielle and Adrian are so great together! They definitely have some hot chemistry. I don't want to provide any spoilers but it really is a wonderful book! I hope you decide to read it!!. (review on Amazon)

If you are ready to read a book that is the best of the best, then this is your book right here. WOW oh WOW did Olivia write one heck of a FANTASTIC book. I wish I had run into a man like Adrian when I was growing up on the farm. He sounds like a major HUNK I would have devoured. Danielle is a really wonderful character as well. I think this book is perfect and I will reread it again sometime. (review on Amazon)

This was a story that immediately drew you in. We follow Danielle who, after the breakdown of her marriage and on the advice of her friend Savannah, goes to a ranch that is also a retreat resort. She meets Adrian, the owner there, and he has a brother, an identical twin, who stays there for privacy and other problems and no one is allowed to know. They have chemistry and attraction from the start. What happens when she sees him or so she thinks because she doesn't know that he is half of an identical twin, but it is Brian instead of Adrain. Will she find out in time that he is not Adrian or will it be too late and will she leave because she thinks he cannot be trusted or always acts as if he does not know her? Will he explain to her that it is his twin brother and not him? A wonderful page turner! (review on Amazon)

Blurbs:

I come to this special ranch with a tall, muscular, and deliciously tanned owner to heal my old wounds, but I end up pregnant instead.

Despite initial frustrations with the hot weather and their electronic cleansing policies, the allure of the ranch draws me in.

The charismatic rancher, with his captivating gaze and smile, melts every cell in my body.

In between my therapy sessions and ranch activities, I play bedroom with my hunk of a rancher.

He's everything I've ever wanted in a man, until he's not.

One minute he can't resist me, the next minute, he doesn't even recognize me.

His extreme mood swings, oscillating between passion and coldness, stir anger and frustration within me.

n within me.

I can't take it anymore—not again. I thought he was different.

I'm leaving, and I don't want to have anything to do with him.

Until he shows up at my door, revealing a shocking truth.

Anxious to let him know that I've taken a piece of him as a souvenir.

Yet, we are far from prepared for the unforeseen surprise that awaits us.

Content Warning: This book includes spicy content. Reader discretion is advised.

Surprise Babies For My Billionaire Rancher: A Mistaken Identity Vacation Romance

Chapter One: Danielle

"Excuse me, Miss? I need to pass."

I mutter something under my breath and ignore the soft voice that beckons me back to the land of the living.

Then someone touches my shoulder. I jolt awake, my vision swimming in and out of focus.

When it clears, I recognize the overhead compartments and the smell of airplane peanuts.

I blink, then I realize that the man sitting next to me is leaning sideways between us, an apologetic look on his face.

I rub a hand over my face and chase away the sleep. With a yawn I unfasten my seatbelt. Once I do, I stand up and move into the aisle between the seats.

With a smile, the older man with salt and pepper hair, and tight lines around his eyes, shimmies out of the seat next to me and into the aisle.

I sink back into my seat, and my hand moves to the drool collecting near the side of my mouth.

Hastily, I wipe it away with a cocktail napkin and squeeze my eyes shut. I hear another murmured voice.

When I open my eyes, I see the flight attendant in a black and white uniform two seats in front of me, a rehearsed smile in place.

Sighing, I sit up straighter and fold my hands in my lap.

I still have no idea what I'm doing on a plane or if going to this retreat is a good idea. Good idea or not, I know it's a little too late to change my mind.

After all, we're less than an hour away from our destination.

The plane gives a slight jolt, and I dig my nails into the armrests on either side of me.

Is this how I'm going to die? In an airplane owned by an airline whose name I can't remember? Before I even get the chance to make it to my retreat?

Stop being so negative. You're on vacation, remember? This is your chance to relax, unwind, and forget all about your life in the city. And about everything you've left behind.

Including an ex-husband who left me multiple messages before I got on the plane. And I already know I'll have many more when we land.

The thought leaves me with a bad taste in my mouth.

Ironic. This is from a guy who spent our entire three years of marriage ignoring me and only acknowledging me when he needed something. Now he won't leave me alone.

I can't deny the relief I feel at having finally plucked up the courage to leave him.

Being stuck in a loveless marriage has taken its toll on me. How I hate that I've wasted so much time on the wrong man.

As if I could've made Trevor into someone he wasn't.

You wasted too much time on that asshole. It's time to put him out of your mind. Kick him out of your heart once and for all.

The plane gives another jolt, and I press my lips together.

Then the fasten seatbelt sign comes on.

Out of the corner of my eye, I see several people return to their seats, wearing anxious expressions.

Moments later, I see the guy from the seat next to me coming back down the aisle.

Droplets of water slid down his face, and a furrow lies between his brows. I tuck my legs in closer and straighten my back.

When he squeezes past, I smell cheap soap and sweat mixed.

He pulls the seatbelt on and tilts his head in my direction. "You alright? You were really out of it."

I lick my dry lips. "Yeah, I'm fine. Sorry if it took you a while to wake me up. I didn't sleep much last night."

Or any night for the past three years.

I've been living off of coffee, anxiety, and the stress of my job for so long that I'm not sure I even remember how to be a functional adult.

Still, I have hope that it's not always going to be like this.

I have, after all, spent the past few months gluing myself back together and figuring out my next move.

Being at Savannah's felt good, particularly when I realized how stifled I felt. But I knew I couldn't hide in her apartment forever.

After weeks of moping around in my ratty old pajamas and eating soggy cereal and ice cream over the sink, it's time for me to start facing the outside world.

And with plenty of vacation days saved up, and nothing else to do with my time, I know that Savannah is right.

I do need a change of pace and scenery.

Which is why I'm hoping the Four Elements Ranch in Montana is exactly what the doctor ordered. Apparently, this ranch is a very unusual one.

According to Savannah, the owner of the ranch serves his guests personally.

And the ranch has a therapist and a psychiatrist who work with guests who need them and to overcome whatever they need to overcome.

I was quite intrigued. The on-site therapist, it definitely made it easier for me to decide to experience this unique therapeutic retreat for myself, up close and personal.

But still, I have my doubts.

With a sigh, I squeeze my eyes shut and roll back my shoulders.

The captain's voice comes on, low and soothing, but I can't make out what he says.

It isn't until the plane begins to shift and descend that my eyes fly open, and I stare at the other side of the aisle.

People are shifting anxiously in their seats. My stomach drops.

Finally, the plane touches the ground with a shudder. I hear the familiar screeching sound and brace myself for the plane to come to a halt.

When it does, a thin sheen of sweat covers my forehead, and I can't deny how relieved I am. I never liked this part of flying.

Shortly after, the seatbelt sign blinks off, and several people get out of their seats at once.

Luckily, my neighbor isn't one of them.

I study the people who retrieve their luggage from the overhead compartments. Then I fish my phone out of my pocket and take it off of airplane mode.

Predictably, several messages come in at once, all of them from a furious and pushy Trevor demanding to know where I am.

With a roll of my eyes, I ignore them all, pull up my contacts, and dial Savanna's number.

"Hey. How was the flight?"

"I slept through most of it," I reply. "The good news is that it's been a while since I've slept that deeply. The bad news is that I'm pretty sure I pulled something in my neck."

Savannah chuckles. "You always think you've pulled something. Just put a heat pack or an ice pack on it when you get there."

"That's if they have them." I shove my hair out of my face and peer out the window at the relatively empty runway, where the plane is still idling. "Remind me again why we thought it was a good idea for me to go to a ranch of all places."

"Because they have a good package. And you get the chance to work on your issues. Not just escape them."

I sigh. "I hate it when you're right."

"If it makes you feel any better, I miss you already," Savannah offers. "And so does Skittles. Right, baby?"

Skittles' familiar meow fills my ears, and a wave of longing hits me.

What am I even doing on this plane?

I'm not supposed to be in Montana, waiting to be cut off from the rest of the world for a whole month.

I want to be back home, in Savannah's apartment, with Skittles purring on my lap, a tub of half-eaten ice cream by my side, and a trashy TV playing in the background.

That's the kind of therapy and healing I need.

But I know if I fly back, Savannah will drag me here herself.

It's too late for me to change my mind, so I might as well see this through.

I clear my throat. "I miss you guys too. Don't watch The Voice without me, okay? Just record the episodes, and we'll watch them together when I get back."

"I don't know, Dee. That's a lot of episodes."

"What happened to being loyal?"

"It doesn't extend to TV shows," Savannah jokes before her voice drifts away then and comes back on. "Anyway, what's happening? Are you off the plane yet?"

"I'm getting off now. Let me call you right back."

Out of the corner of my eye, I spot a flash of movement, and the door to the plane opens. One by one, the other passengers trickle out, moving forward at a snail's pace.

When most of the plane has cleared, I stand up and retrieve my small bag.

Then I flash my neighbor a small smile and realize he's also on his phone, murmuring in a quiet voice.

As I make my way down the aisle, I take in the blankets thrown haphazardly, the empty wrappers thrown on seats, and the crumbs of food on the floor.

On my way off the plane, I give the flight attendants my best smile.

Despite the bags under their eyes, many of them smile back.

A blast of hot air hits me as I take the stairs two at a time. At the bottom, a bus is waiting. It whooshes open, and I breathe a sigh of relief when I realize it's got AC.

Smiling, I step in, wheeling my bag behind me. A few more people climb onto the bus, all of us standing and waiting.

After the last passenger climbs on, the doors whoosh to close, and it jerks to life.

I sit down and dial Savannah.

"I'm on the way to the terminal right now," I say when she picks up.

"Good, so how does everything look?"

"You do realize I'm not there yet, right?"

"Right, yeah."

"Sav, it's not too late to join me," I murmur, before patting my pockets for my earpiece. I place one in either ear and shove my phone into my pocket. "I did book a room with two beds in case you changed your mind."

"That's sweet, Dee, but you need to do this on your own. Besides, I'm buried under mountains of assignments. They're not going to correct themselves; you know."

"I'm sure no one would mind if you were a little late..."

Savannah snorts, and I hear the familiar beep of the microwave. "You've obviously never taught a day in your life. The second the students handed in the assignments, they started nagging me about when I'll post their grades."

My lips lift into a half smile. "Lucky for them it usually doesn't take you long. Since you don't have a life."

"Fuck you very much."

In the distance, the airport looms, a thick plume of heat shimmering around it.

The doors to the bus dart open, and I get off, wheeling the bag behind me. I'm already sweating in the few seconds it takes me to cross through the double doors.

A blast of cold air hits me, and I smile.

Then I follow the signs to the conveyor belt, the rest of the passengers trailing behind me.

"Hello? Sav?"

"....signal....phone....water...."

I roll my eyes. "Please don't tell me you dropped your phone in the sink again. I thought you were going to figure out a way to stop doing that."

With glass windows on either side of me overlooking a packed airport runway and several pulsing neon signs, I'm able to find my way easily.

I move from one auto-walk to the next, rushing past rows and rows of brightly colored shops on either side of me.

A few vendors even wave at me, but I ignore them all and make a beeline for the baggage claim area.

My shoes squeak against linoleum floors. I'm nervous when I round the corner and spot several conveyor belts.

Quickly, I study the screen and manage to figure out which one has my luggage. Then I wander over to it and shove a hand into my pocket.

"I didn't drop my phone in the water." Savanna's voice is finally back, and it's clearer than before. "Skittles pushed it into the sink."

I snort. "What did you do? Did you forget to pet her right?"

"I know you don't buy this because she normally behaves around you, but Skittles can actually be very mean. The other day she hissed at me because I tried to take her food bowl away."

"Maybe you shouldn't have taken the bowl away."

"She wasn't eating anymore, and you remember what the vet said about her weight."

As I wait for the conveyor belt to come to life, I shift from one foot to the other. "I'm sure she'll forgive you eventually."

Savannah sighs. "Or you'll come back home and discover my half-eaten body in the bathroom."

"You really need to stop listening to those true crime podcasts." I shake my head and stand up straighter. "All they do is freak you out and leave you paranoid."

"I can't help it. Besides, I'm not like you. I need to know what's happening in the world."

"I know what's happening in the world, thank you very much," I reply, a little too quickly. "I've just, you know, been busy."

"Babe, I know that pretending to be in love with Trevor must've been exhausting, but you know you don't have to make excuses anymore, right? That's part of what the retreat is for. I'm glad they actually have a few therapists on site."

I grimace. "Why did you have to remind me? I never should've let you convince me to do this."

Especially because I'm not comfortable talking to a stranger about how my marriage fell apart after only three years to boot.

I feel like a failure, and I have no idea how to come back from it.

Even though I still have a semi-successful career as a journalist, part of me wonders if that's going to fall apart too.

The rest of the world moved on while I was stuck in limbo.

When I was stuck trying to win the love of a man who can't love anyone but himself.

Why the fuck did I waste so much time on him?

Because you married him. And you don't like giving up. Even when you know you should.

"Babe, there's nothing wrong with going to therapy. You need someone to talk to."

"I've got you."

"I'm not a licensed therapist, and unless you start paying me—"

"I can do that."

"I was kidding," Savannah continues. I can hear the exasperation in her voice. "You do realize that even if you did pay me, it still won't work. I'm not supposed to be the one helping you."

"Then let me eat ice cream and binge-watch The Bachelorette. That's all the therapy I need."

"You can discuss that with your therapist. Anyway, look I've got to go. I've got leftover pizza to eat and a whole lot of assignments that need correcting. And I've got a pop quiz to prepare for."

"Alright, alright. Jeez, I get it."

"You're going to be fine. Message me when you've got your bag. Is someone picking you up?"

I stare at the bags spinning in a large circle and sigh. "Yeah, but I'm starting to think I should've sprung for something fancier. And fucking Trevor should've paid for this whole thing. He's the one who needs therapy."

"I agree. But unless you can figure out a way to forge his signature or something, it's all on you, girl."

I run a hand over my face. "I hate it when you make sense. Okay, I'll message you before I get into the car. Just remember that I won't be able to use my phone much. They have some policy about laptops and phones. We're only allowed to use them for like an hour a day."

"True! I forgot about that. In that case, I'm so glad I didn't come! Talk to you later, babe."

"Talk to you later."

When Savannah hangs up, I glance around at the cluster of people waiting. The knots in my stomach tighten.

I miss my best friend already. And I really hate that I'm out here on my own. Still, I try to convince myself that I'm doing the right thing.

Between the therapy and a near-total social media purge, I'm hoping this retreat delivers on everything it's promising.

Including rest and rejuvenation.

Because I desperately need to feel like I'm not floating around, aimless and lost.

A part of me can already hear Trevor's critical voice in my head. Dragging me through the mud like he always did.

Another part of me keeps reliving the day I woke up to his horrible mess.

When I saw Trevor in his den, leftover food and take-out boxes littering every surface, a pair of headphones pulled low over his head, something in me broke.

I realized that I'd had enough.

I'm still not sure what it was about seeing Trevor like that that made me snap.

All I know is that racing back up the stairs to pack my bag and message Savannah felt right.

Leaving my dead marriage was one of the best decisions I've ever made.

But I can't help but worry about what the future has in store for me.

And why it has to begin in Montana of all places.

Read more for FREE on Kindle Unlimited:

https://www.amazon.com/dp/B0CQX25K9 Direct Amazon Link

https://books2read.com/u/4Aazzq Universal Link to Amazon

·♥·♥·♥·♥·♥·

"My Secret Baby With The Billionaire" is part of a BOX SET of 3 stand-alone books.

"Off Limits Silver Fox Billionaire: A Second Chance Secret Baby Romance Box Set"

1. My Secret Baby With The Billionaire: An Age Gap Second Chance Romance

2. My Bad Boy Protector: A Friends To Lovers Second Chance Romance https://books2read.com/u/3k91BK Universal Link to Amazon

3. The Billionaire's Secret Intentions: An Age Gap Brother's Best Friends Romance https://books2read.com/u/br9vBA Universal Link to Amazon

Read more for FREE on Kindle Unlimited:

https://www.amazon.com/dp/B0CN2G2B6Q Box Set Link

https://books2read.com/u/bzroBj Universal Link to Amazon site for the Box Set

· ♥ · ♥ · ♥ · ♥ · ♥ ·

Here is a sneak peek of the 3rd book:

"The Billionaire's Secret Intentions: An Age Gap Brother's Best Friend Romance"

https://www.amazon.com/dp/B0CHXZ3TF3

https://books2read.com/u/br9vBA Universal Link

Reviews:

wow such an excellent read. Kaylee has had a long time crush on Ian. They have not seen each other for several years. When they meet again, the electricity zapping between them is palpable. Are Kaylee and Ian destined to be together? Will Kaylee forgive Ian after he reveals his secret? Can Kaylee open her heart once again after being heartbroken from a previous relationship? Does Ian finally find out the mystery regarding his Father? I TOTALLY recommend this 5++ winner to find out the answers to these questions and more. I didn't want to put it down it's that good. I'd give it 20s if I could. This ebook is filled with family drama, excitement, secrets, criminal activity, payback, hot intense passionate moments, and forbidden love. So what do you get when you add a mystery about a parent, a cheating ex, and a coworker who steals? Why you get so much more spice. Whew! This very talented author deserves a standing ovation for her superb writing. She gets you so involved in her characters lives that you find yourself giving them advice or a good talking to. I just had to give some advice for Kaylee to hear. Tell him how you feel and remember to listen! I know that without a doubt you will love this ebook as much as I do. I most definitely encourage you to get this surefire hit.You won't be disappointed I promise!□. (review on Amazon)

read daily and this compared to other books I have read this past week deserves a 5 star review. Building passion, a dramatic family twist, and great kid characters, make this book a fantastic brain break. (review on Amazon)

Kaylee owns a bakery which is having financial problems due to an ex employee stealing her recipes and opening another bakery close by. Kaylee's childhood crush, her brother's best friend, Ian is back in town. When Ian learns of Kaylee's bakery problems he offers to help her rebrand her product.

Kaylee and Ian become closer as they work together to rebrand the bakery. They both have trust issues that will have to be overcome if they go forward in their relationship. What secrets are being kept? Does Ian betray Kaylee? Will they be able to move forward?

The Billionaire's Secret Intentions has plenty of drama, suspense, secrets, romance, twists and turns to keep you interested until the end. (review on Amazon)

Blurbs:

My heart sank when I heard that he's back in town.

The door swings open, revealing him - my childhood crush - tall and incredibly gorgeous.

The sight of his chiseled physique takes my breath away.

He's an accomplished self-made billionaire with an irresistible charm that could win anyone over.

His unwavering attention on me becomes an addictive force, leaving me hungry for more.

The more I have him the more I want him.

A bakery I've poured my heart into is struggling.

His proposal to rescue it from financial ruin means only one thing, spending more time together.

The concept of him settling for a quiet hometown life creates a disbelief in me.

Doubts arise about his true intentions in being back.

A painful reality strikes me as I uncover the truth.

My world shatters, trusting him appears to be a big mistake.

The only way forward is to pull away, but I'm already deeply in love with him.

Content Warning: This book includes spicy content. Reader discretion is advised.

"The Billionaire's Secret Intentions: An Age Gap Brother's Best Friend Romance"

Chapter One: Kaylee

"How do you know if a boy likes you?"

The last scone almost falls from my hand as I turn to my six-year-old niece, Brooke. She's seated on the chair closest to me, peering at me with curiosity through her large green eyes. Her raven-black hair, so similar to mine, cups her cheeks.

"What?"

Brooke closes her book. "Is it true that when a boy pulls your hair and says mean things, he likes you?"

Dropping my scone on the table, I pull out a chair and lean forward.

"If someone likes you, they're kind to you. They want you to be happy. They don't want to make you cry."

"Like Logan." She cocks her head. "Mom said he made you cry a lot."

An ache spreads through my chest, and I shut my eyes, inhaling sharply. The dark swirling thoughts threaten to come up, but I shove them down and smile at my niece.

Before I can think of something to say, the door opens and Elena rushes in. Her hair's messy, and there are dark circles under her eyes.

One glance at her daughter, and her face breaks into a smile. Brooke runs into her arms. Elena strokes her daughter's hair and smiles tiredly at me.

"Thanks for watching her. The meeting took longer than I expected."

I hand Brooke the scone. "We just had a lovely conversation. Didn't we, Brooke?"

Elena straightens and holds Brooke's hand.

"She pestered you with questions, huh?"

I laugh. "A few."

Her phone buzzes. She stares at the screen and mutters.

"I have to go." Elena holds me in a one-armed hug. "We'll talk about this," she says and waves a hand around my shop, uttering, "later." Grabbing Brooke's bag, she nudges her toward the door. "I love you!"

Brooke echoes the same thing. I wave.

"Love you too."

"Don't forget to give Dylan the book." Elena pauses at the door. "I'm sure he'll notice if I don't return it tonight, even if he's preoccupied with his best friend."

My brows furrow. "Do they have one of their online game sessions again?"

"Online games? Of course not. Ian's back."

My mouth falls open.

Wait. What?

"Got to go. See you at dinner!"

I stare at the door for a long time after they've left before lowering myself to the nearest chair. Ian is back? After what – seven years?

My phone buzzes—a text from Elena.

Don't forget the book!

Then another text.

Let's talk about her on Sunday.

Her.

And just like that, my mood sours. Sweeping the shop with my gaze, I grab my colorful tote bag from behind the counter.

It's a tiny place: a show-glass with some baked goods, a few tables, bright yellow walls with little drawings of all the pastries I make, and little else. It's like a tiny portion of the universe I've carved out for myself over the past year.

From the first moment I stepped into the shop, I just knew this was where I was supposed to be.

Will I have to give this up?

Shoving the thoughts aside, I lock up the shop and drive to Dylan's house. I'm on his porch ten minutes later, raising my fist to knock. There's the sound of a loud familiar laugh near the door. Bracing myself, I plaster a smile on my face.

The door opens and my jaw drops. He's…different. Taller than I remember. A black shirt stretches around his broad shoulders. A five o' clock shadow graces his jaw, and when I look up, his ocean-blue eyes are on mine.

Ian's smile fades and his eyes narrow.

"Damn."

A tingle shoots through my spine. What's that in his eyes — admiration? Awe? Surprise?

Ian's gaze rakes over me slowly, heating me everywhere his eyes land. His eyes...they're just like they used to be. Intense.

Like they can see beneath the layers of my skin. An image of my appearance flashes through my head, and I shift from foot to foot. I'm in shorts and a black jacket over a pink top, and my face is bare.

I learned long ago that makeup and baking don't go well together. It's not like I need it. Not since I traded skirts and heels for an apron and a chef's hat.

"Kaylee!"

I inhale sharply. His voice has gotten deeper somehow. More...*something*. I don't know. Combing a hand through my hair, I swallow and clear my throat.

"Y-you're back."

Stating the obvious. No shit he's back.

"Yes," he says softly. "I am."

I glance away from him for a split second.

"Welcome back."

Wow. How articulate.

Ian leans against the doorframe and crosses his arms. His muscles bulge. He's definitely gotten more chiseled since I last saw him. My mouth is dry.

I tear my gaze away from his arms and stare at the chairs on the porch. This is ridiculous. Why do I suddenly feel like I'm a kid with a crush again?

I'm twenty-four for goodness' sake, yeah, I was seventeen when he left, yet here I am standing in front of my brother's best friend with flamed cheeks and a too-big grin plastered on my face.

The sound of music and my brother's singing drifts into my ears. He whistles loudly and laughs. He's probably too busy talking to his girlfriend to notice my arrival.

"You look different," Ian says.

And you look so much hotter than I remember.

"I cut my hair."

Suddenly self conscious, I tug at the ends of my chopped hair. I cut it right after I vowed to get a divorce. My waist-length hair was one of the things that Logan loved — so chopping it off was an act or rebellion.

I no longer wanted to be the woman he wanted. I was shedding the layers into becoming the woman *I* wanted.

Not that Ian would know that.

"It suits you."

A smile tugs at my lips. "Thanks."

"Elena?" Dylan says, footsteps nearing the door. "You brought my book?"

Ian takes a step back as Dylan sticks his head out. Average height, with long dark hair packed up in a tiny ponytail at the nape and a stud on his ear, my brother looks more like a college freshman than a man in his mid-thirties.

He's always been the type to defy the odds and go after what he wants, even if it's not what's typical. One reason for his many altercations with Dad. He glances behind me and frowns.

"She didn't come, did she? I knew I shouldn't have trusted her to keep to our agreement."

"Relax, Dylan." I whip out the book from my old tote bag and raise if up. "Here's your prized possession."

Dylan grins and snatches the book from my grasp. "Sweet." He glances between me and Ian. "Oh yeah. Ian's back." Then he hurries into the house.

I hold Ian's gaze, and we both laugh.

"There should've been an announcement in the paper or something."

Ian chuckles. "I'm not one for dramatic entrances."

"How long are you back?"

We've finally gotten past the initial awkwardness. Good.

Ian pauses. "I'm not sure yet. Depends."

Before I can ask, he says,

"You coming in?"

"Erm." I glance at my car. I have nothing to do all night aside from obsessing over my accounts, scrolling through my feed, and maybe soaking in my bathtub with a glass of wine and my favorite book. And then relaxing in the bath for an hour before finally going to bed.

But now, watching my brother's childhood friend in front of me, those options don't seem as appealing.

"Yeah sure." I nod. "I think I'll crash your party."

He waves me in. "There's not much to crash. Just two guys, a couple drinks, and some video games. You still play?"

Dylan's house is just like him. Eccentric. Each wall is a different color – brown, white, cream, black.

A studio chair in the corner, with a camera. Large paintings hanging on the walls. A beautiful oil painting right above the fireplace. A furry rug drapes the floor. Rows of books take up more than half the white wall, along with action figures he's had since he was twelve years old.

Dylan whistles from a room – a no-go area. Invites only. The only person allowed to enter that room uninvited is…well, Ian. Dylan never lets anyone see the paintings he's working on until it's perfect and in his gallery.

"Err, play?"

"Video games."

I drop my bag on a couch and turn to Ian.

"It's been so long." I haven't played video games since college…the night I met Logan. I blink away the memory. "I don't think I can still play."

Ian cocks his head. "You used to love it."

Laughing, I shake my head. "Things change."

His expression turns serious and he cocks his head, studying me intently.

"How have you been, Kaylee?"

The question stuns me into silence. His eyes bore into mine, pinning me to the spot. I can't speak. Ian's gaze doesn't waver.

Another thing that hasn't changed about him: he's always been the type to ask how are you and *actually* want to listen. To him, it's not just a greeting, a thing people say to make small talk. He actually wants to know.

"I'm —"

"Okay! I'm not going back there until tomorrow," Dylan says, popping out of his studio. He wipes his hands with a napkin. "I forgot myself in there for a minute. Sorry about that. Where were we?"

"The part where you get the drinks," Ian says, lowering himself to a couch. My gaze lands on his hands. Large firm hands. Staring at them triggers a vivid memory. Those large hands, wrapped around my waist. Helping me find my balance, while my head swam with the aftereffects of alcohol...

" – standing like that?"

I blink him into focus. "Um, what?"

"Yeah. That." Dylan snaps his fingers and hurries away.

Ian pats the space next to him. "Will you sit down or you prefer hovering above me?"

"I can hardly *hover* above you." I laugh, taking a seat next to him. We're close. His thigh is just an inch from mine. His scent overpowers my senses, and I inhale deeply. He doesn't smell the same. Of course, he doesn't. A lot of things have changed about him.

He drapes his arm over the headrest, and I raise my eyes to meet his. He's grinning. I smile back.

"What?"

"It's good to see you, Kaylee."

I swallow. "It's err...good to see you too."

Geez. Why am I being so tongue-tied? Yes, he's *the* Ian Reynolds. Billionaire and serial entrepreneur with his fair share of awards. But before he became that, he was just Ian. My brother's best friend. That was it.

"Good."

He pats my thigh. It's supposed to be a casual gesture – and maybe to him it is – but his touch sends a thrill through me, and I suck in a breath. His fingers are warm.

"Here they are!" Dylan appears holding drinks. "Pick your poisons." He connects Ian's phone to a speaker and puts on some music. "Time to celebrate my homeboy's return to where it all began." His phone rings. "Be right back."

"He'll probably be gone for an hour," I say, holding up a bottle. "He'll spend the whole day talking to Jessie if he can."

Ian pours me a drink. We chink glasses. I down the drink in two gulps. He stares at me, and I laugh.

"That was fast."

I smirk. "I'm not sixteen anymore."

His expression changes, and we fall silent. I know what he's thinking – I'm thinking it too.

Read more for FREE on Kindle Unlimited:

https://www.amazon.com/dp/B0CHXZ3TF3 Stand-alone Book Link

https://books2read.com/u/br9vBA Universal Link

·♥·♥·♥·♥·♥·

Get your FREE copy of my book:

"Off Limits NAVY SEAL: An Age Gap Best Friend's Brother Romance"

https://dl.bookfunnel.com/p5b9qs6g5b

That night when I slammed into a wall with a heartbeat and a pair of green eyes, my life took a sudden turn.

Soon after, I found myself in the back seat of his car, losing my V-Card.

To my surprise, the man with whom I had fogged the car windows with that night, was my best friend's estranged brother.

And when I agreed to vacation with my friend's family, I didn't think he would be sleeping in the room next to mine.

This bad boy and ex- NAVY SEAL definitely adds an exciting twist to this family getaway.

Every time he enters the premises, I'm hit with a rush of sensations, his scent alone sends shivers down my spine.

His sister warned me that he was cold-hearted and prone to breaking hearts, but I'm unable to resist him.

I find myself sneaking into his bed late at night, wrinkling his sheets.

Now, I question whether it's love or just a temporary game.

My heart aches with uncertainty, yet this secret relationship ignites a passion I can hardly control.

Visit and follow Olivia Mack's author page on Amazon for more books and notifications about new releases.

https://www.amazon.com/author/oliviamack